Dear Story Pr

My dad says you'll never read this letter a̶n̶d̶
you don't care about children. All you crave is
attention. But I don't believe him.

Michael and I think you're beautiful. You remind us
of our mom. She died and went to heaven.
Michael's going there soon to be with her. But
before that happens, he wants to spend a day with
you.

Being with you would make him the happiest boy
on earth, and we could prove to our dad that the
contest isn't a gimik. Sorry, Story Princess, but I
don't know how to spell some of the words. I don't
know what a bee grade actress is, but I know you
love children because your voice is nice.

My dad says you act different when you go home. I
don't believe him, so would you please think about
it?

Your friends,

Peter Wolfe, 8 years old.
Michael Wolfe, 5 years old.

P.S. If Michael wins, could I come too? Thanks.

Rebecca Winters, an American writer and mother of four, is a graduate of the University of Utah who has also studied overseas at schools in Switzerland and France, including the Sorbonne. She is currently teaching French and Spanish to junior high school students. Despite her busy schedule, Rebecca always finds time to write. She's already researching the background for her next Harlequin Romance!

Books by Rebecca Winters

HARLEQUIN ROMANCE
2953—BLIND TO LOVE
3047—FULLY INVOLVED

THE STORY PRINCESS

Rebecca Winters

Harlequin Books

TORONTO • NEW YORK • LONDON
AMSTERDAM • PARIS • SYDNEY • HAMBURG
STOCKHOLM • ATHENS • TOKYO • MILAN

ISBN 0-373-03090-8

Harlequin Romance first edition November 1990

To Beverly and Louise,
who've been my inspiration

CHAPTER ONE

"...So REMEMBER, boys and girls. The deadline is Friday at midnight. It's still not too late to enter the contest. All you have to do is send a letter to me, the Story Princess, telling why you'd like to spend the day with me. Address your letter to KLPC Television Station, Box 9000, Seattle, Washington. The boy or girl who sends the winning letter will be my guest at the studio, with a chance to perform on one of my weekly shows. The winner will be notified by mail. The contest is open to children ten years of age or younger."

Peter Wolfe wrote the address on a piece of paper while his little brother, Michael, turned off the TV so they could concentrate. "Lots of kids will be sending her letters, Mike. Ours will have to be really good to win."

"Let's tell her she has the most prettiest voice in the whole world, and that she's the most beautifulest princess in the world."

"Mom looked a little bit like her."

"I don't remember Mommy. I wish the Story Princess was our mom. She could tell us stories every night. Write in the letter that we don't have a mommy and that's why we want to win."

Peter thought Mike's idea sounded pretty good, and he began to compose their letter. Mike lay down beside him in front of the fire and watched.

"You're wasting your time," their father commented. "The entire state of Washington will be entering that contest. The child who wins will have to be on the verge of death."

Peter craned his neck to stare at his father, who sat reading the newspaper. Once in a while his dad sounded irritated, like now. Maybe they shouldn't have mentioned their mom. "Is that true, Dad?"

"Afraid so, Pete. The contest is a publicity gimmick to sell more records and entice more viewers. A dying child's request will add drama. But the whole idea is ridiculous because the Story Princess is already a household fixture. Children's Playhouse Record Company doesn't need more money. It's indecent."

"What's indecent?" Michael stared wide-eyed at his father.

"Like the way you ate all your chocolate bells on Christmas morning before we opened presents and didn't tell me until after I rushed you to the hospital," their father murmured behind his paper. "That's indecent."

"Oh." He gave Peter an embarrassed look. "I still wish we'd win. We'd get to be on TV. Maybe she'd let us act out 'The Gingerbread Man.'"

"She's already done that one. The winner will get to do a new story," Peter reasoned.

The sound of the newspaper being tossed onto the coffee table brought both children's blond heads around. "In all likelihood the winner will have a few lines in the chorus section." Their dad rose to his full six-foot height and stretched. "Neither of you is old enough to understand that although she may have the face and voice of an angel, in reality she's a grade-B actress who needs an audience to exist. The point is, she's got what it takes to make money for the record company and the television studio."

Peter watched his dad scoop Mike from the floor and give him a bear hug before setting him on his broad shoulders. "Mike—remember that in all probability the Story Princess doesn't even like children. Don't make her out to be more than she is. After the show is over she goes home like everyone else. You only see what she's like in front of the TV cameras. She could be a vastly different proposition when she's not acting."

"Well, I love her!" Michael's voice quavered after their dad had delivered his quelling remarks. "I still want to win."

"So do thousands of other children. That's why the whole thing is so ridiculous. Now it's time for bed. Let's go up."

Peter felt his dad's hand tousle his hair. "Will you turn out the lights, son? That'll save Mrs. Maughan the trouble."

"Yes, Dad." Peter did as he was asked, then followed them up the staircase to the room he shared with Michael, overlooking Port Orchard Bay. Long after they'd brushed their teeth, said their prayers and hopped into bed, Peter still lay awake wondering what they'd done to annoy their father.

As he reflected on everything his dad had said, an idea began to take hold. Unable to lie there any longer, Peter crept out of bed and went over to the desk to write his letter to the Story Princess. He didn't finish until he heard the foghorn of the midnight ferry returning from Seattle.

"HERE'S THE LAST BATCH of mail, Miss Loring."

Domini raised her eyes from the pile of letters spread across her desk. "Thank heaven! Put them in the basket, Marge. I'll get to them later."

As soon as the redheaded receptionist had closed the door, Domini sat back in the swivel chair, exhausted. The idea of reading another heartrending letter was almost more than she could bear. She hadn't approved of the contest in the first place, but she'd been overruled by her producer, Carter Phillips, and by the station management. She sighed, glancing at the latest stack of mail. Appearing on a weekly TV show, on top of making records, had created a lot of publicity but this contest was something else again. How could she possibly choose the winning entry? Almost all the hundreds of letters she'd read were priceless little masterpieces.

She reached for the basket and began reading the final entries, vowing never to be placed in this situation again. At least the deadline had passed, she thought with relief. According to the Post Office, the contest had generated more mail than Santa Claus.

Carter had acted positively euphoric over the response and had hired a group of people to screen the mail that poured in, but Domini had to make the final choice from those letters passed on to her, most of them written by children in problem homes, or seriously ill youngsters who'd needed the help of an adult to write their entries.

Domini immersed herself in work for another couple of hours, unaware that the building had long since emptied. Unfortunately, in the two weeks the contest had run, she hadn't yet come across a letter that truly stood out from the rest.

Through bleary eyes she noted the Bremerton post-mark on the next envelope in the basket. Deciding this would be the last one for tonight, she opened it, but her mind was on the prospect of going home to a hot shower and bed. The letter was written in a child's hand, but the printing revealed surprising uniformity even if the sentences slanted as they reached the side of the page.

She smiled as she imagined the thousands of children sitting down to write their letters. It touched her to realize so many youngsters still loved the world of make-believe in spite of the technological age.

Dear Story Princess,
My dad says you'll never read this letter and that you don't care about children. All you crave is attention. But I don't believe him.

Domini's smile faded as she continued to read, sitting straight in her chair, fully awake by now.

Michael and I think you're beautiful, and that you have the most beautiful voice in the world. You remind us of our mom. She died and went to heaven. Michael's going there soon to be with her. But before that happens, he wants to spend the day with you.

Her gaze was riveted to the rest of the letter.

Being with you would make him the happiest boy on earth, and we could prove to our dad that the contest isn't a gimik. Sorry, Story Princess, but I don't know how to spell some of the words. I don't know what a bee grade actress is, but I know you love children because your voice is nice.

My dad says you act different when you go home. I don't believe him, so would you please think about it?

Your friends, Peter and Michael Wolfe

P.S. If Michael wins, could I come too? Thanks, Peter, 8 years old. Michael, 5 years old.

P.P.S. Could Mrs. Maughan come, too? She takes care of us.

Domini's eyes widened in astonishment. She didn't know whether to laugh or cry. The letter was an original, and the children's father the original cynic! How dare he say those kinds of things to his own innocent children!

Domini got up from her desk abruptly, the letter still in hand. Perhaps the man could be forgiven since he'd lost his wife and was about to lose one of his boys. The situation couldn't be more tragic. Still, his judgmental attitude irritated her. The fact that the man wasn't so far off with his B-grade actress comment stung.

Years earlier she could have been an opera singer—something her doctor father had wanted for her—but in the end she didn't pursue it because she couldn't commit herself to such a demanding career. This man's observation was near enough to the truth to hurt just a little.

She reread the letter. It appeared the father had run out of hope. Perhaps he'd run out of money as well. Hospital bills could soar into the thousands of dollars, especially with a long-term illness.

She paced the floor. What that family needed was a miracle. Her thoughts turned to the boy, Peter, and the burden he carried. Older than his years, he was watching out for his little brother's happiness, obviously aware that his father was too overcome with grief to indulge in flights of fantasy. The boy's wish that she think about choosing his letter tugged at her heart.

For the first time since Carter had announced the contest, Domini started to feel excited. If visiting the Story Princess would put a little joy in their lives, then the contest was justified. Their household could use a healing balm, and she was in a position to provide it.

All vestiges of fatigue disappeared as she mentally planned her day with the Wolfe boys. She'd entertain them so royally the father wouldn't be able to find fault with a single detail. It would be an unforgettable day. The little boy deserved to have his heart's desire; so did Peter. Without his loving concern for his brother, Domini would never have known anything, never have been able to help. She actually found herself wishing she had the Story Princess's magic powers to prevent the inevitable.

With thoughts and emotions running high, Domini sat down at her typewriter to compose the congratulatory letter. When she finished, she put the letter on Carter's desk. There was a certain satisfaction in knowing that the boys' father would have to admit he'd jumped to some erroneous conclusions about her character and motives. She still smarted from his remark about craving attention. Nothing could be farther from the truth!

Her own father had told her at an early age that her unique voice was a gift—that she had a duty to use it and bring joy to others. Both her parents had encouraged her in music but it was her father who'd sent her to Italy to train as an opera singer after her mother's death. He had visions of her performing Carmen and Aida at the Met one day. But Domini couldn't share those visions and eventually returned to Seattle, much to her father's disappointment, though he did his best not to show it.

She preferred the narrating and singing that went into making the records and she loved her work as a children's performer. Still, she could understand how her parents had wanted to see their only child fulfill her potential in every way. No parents could have been more wonderful and loving. In many respects her childhood had been idyllic. She was exposed to the arts and travel and to the causes her parents espoused. Her talents and interests were vigorously encouraged. But she'd soon realized that she wasn't ambitious enough to carve out a lifetime career for herself. *She did not need the limelight to exist!*

Peter Wolfe's father had a big problem, but after November 10, he'd have to admit he'd been wrong about a few things.

Domini left the production office and headed for her condo on Mercer Island, more lighthearted than she'd been in ages. She knew just the story for the children to help dramatize on her half-hour TV show. That is, if Michael had the physical strength. But no matter, it would be a delightful time for all. She could hardly wait to meet the Wolfe boys. And, if the truth were known, she could hardly wait to prove to their father that he was wrong. She understood exactly how Peter felt!

"THERE HE IS!" Michael shouted, pointing toward the coastal road. Peter dashed out the front door, pulling on his parka, and together the boys ran through the rain to meet the mailman.

Michael had never given up hope that they'd win the contest, but Peter had secretly conceded defeat. It was almost three weeks since he'd mailed the letter and there'd been no reply. Still, his heart raced every time the mail came.

"You guys must be waiting for something important to spend the weekend watching for me." The older man smiled from a weather-beaten face. "What's going on?"

"It's a secret!" Michael piped up.

"I see. Well, let's look in the pouch and find out what's here."

Peter stood back and waited, as the mailman pulled out a bundle secured with rubber bands. It looked like the usual mail for their dad. Expelling a sigh, Peter started to turn toward the house.

"Hey—wait a minute. Could this be it?"

Peter glanced back at the envelope in the man's hand. "I—is it for me?"

"Nobody else. For Peter Wolfe, from KLPC-TV in Seattle."

With a trembling hand Peter took the letter. In his heart he knew it was from the Story Princess. There was only one problem. Maybe she sent everyone letters, telling them they didn't win.

"You don't look very happy," the postman said. "Maybe next time I'll have what you're looking for. So long, boys."

"Bye," they called, but their farewell was lost in the wind blowing off the Sound as they scurried down the steep steps leading from the cliff to the water's edge far below.

"Open it quick!" Michael cried out, pulling shut the door to the boat house. "What does it say?" He followed Peter to the window and watched as his brother pulled the letter from the envelope.

Peter cleared his throat and started to read aloud slowly. "'Dear Peter, thank you for your special letter. I think you must be a remarkable boy to love your brother enough to enter the contest for him.'" Peter felt Michael's eyes fastened on him in rapt attention.

"'I'm writing this letter to inform you that you've won our contest. Congratulations!'" Peter's voice was incredulous.

"Goody!" Michael shrieked, jumping up and down and hugging Peter, who read and then reread the paragraph to make sure he wasn't dreaming. He couldn't believe she'd chosen his letter.

"When will we be on TV?" Michael clutched his arm. "Tomorrow?"

"Just a minute, Mike. Let me finish." Peter read the rest of the letter in silence, experiencing a fleeting sense of guilt over the lie he'd told. It looked like their dad had been right after all, when he'd said the winning child would have to be "on the verge of death." "We're supposed to meet her at the TV studio on November 10. There's a form here dad has to sign to give permission."

Michael let out a whoop of joy. "Let's go up to the house and tell him. He said she didn't like kids, but she does! Now he'll have to believe us!"

"Yeah," Peter echoed his brother with a triumphant gleam in his eye. He was already recovering from his guilt.

"EXCUSE ME," a masculine voice called out as Domini hurried past the reception area, already late for rehearsals with the oratorio society. A glance at her watch told her it was five-thirty. Everyone else at the production company had gone home.

"Yes?" She paused in mid-stride, her breath catching at the sight of a fairly tall, well-built man. Despite his conservative blue pin-striped suit, he projected a raw male strength she couldn't help but notice.

For a moment Domini felt suspended as his assessing glance swept over her from head to toe, lingering on the full curves and rounded hips apparent beneath the forest-green sweater dress she wore. An unfamiliar rush of heat suffused her body as he continued his intimate appraisal.

"I know it's late but I'm looking for the Story Princess. I thought she worked for the television station but found out her office is here at the recording studio. It took me twenty minutes to drive over after discovering my mistake. Could you point me in the right direction?"

Domini studied the striking man who filled the foyer with his presence. The blue silk tie matched his eyes, their color as intense as the indigo of stained glass with the sunshine filtering through. Beneath the glare of the overhead light, his rich brown hair glinted with unmistakable gold highlights. He wasn't a man a woman would forget.

"I'm the Story Princess."

"I find that difficult to believe," he murmured, but the warmth of male admiration in his eyes intensified. He moved closer.

"Let me assure you that you've found her," she said, realizing that he thought the Story Princess was a blonde. Her true identity had never been revealed to the public, a precaution she'd insisted upon to maintain her privacy.

He stopped directly in front of her as his gaze locked with hers. "You're right. You and the Story Princess have the same impossibly green eyes," he said in a quiet tone that sent a delicious chill through her body. "Why do you wear a blond wig when you're even more stunning as a brunette?"

She moistened her lips nervously. "Have you forgotten? All fairy princesses have long flaxen hair. It's the witches whose locks are raven black."

"Well, black or blond, my children consider you the embodiment of perfection."

"Then it's a good thing they don't know me personally."

"But apparently they're going to, according to a certain letter. I'm Dr. Jarod Wolfe, Peter and Michael's father."

This man was the boys' grieving father? Somehow she'd imagined a person quite different from the handsome male whose sensuous appeal reached out to her like a living thing.

"How do you do? I'm Domini Loring," she said, extending a slim, well-manicured hand, which he clasped in a gentle but firm grip. Why a simple handshake should make her aware of his touch clear to the tips of her toes, she had no idea. He finally allowed her to remove her hand. She sucked in a shaky breath. "Are your children happy they won the contest?"

He stared at her for a full minute and she stared back, studying the classic features that made his face so arresting. She felt his gaze travel freely over her delicately arched brows, her slightly almond-shaped green eyes, and linger on the redness of her wide mouth, now fixed in a determined smile.

"Happy isn't exactly the word. It's more like ecstatic. November tenth can't come soon enough for them. Or for me," he admitted wryly. "That's why I'm here. To make sure this isn't some kind of joke."

"I can assure you it's no joke. They won the contest. When I read Peter's letter, I knew I had the winner."

He rubbed the back of his neck in puzzlement. "I have to confess I'm amazed."

"You have a wonderful son, Dr. Wolfe. I was really touched by his love for Michael. It showed a selflessness that I found refreshing." Her voice trembled as she spoke. "I promise to do everything in my power to make their visit perfect."

He blinked, as if surprised by her words. "As long as they get to spend the day with you they'll think they've died and gone to heaven."

She smiled but her eyes misted over. She didn't know how he could say something like that without breaking down completely. Judging from Peter's remarks, though, Dr. Wolfe had a hard streak in his nature that made him an uncompromising realist. He obviously wouldn't allow himself to wallow in self-pity and gave no quarter to anyone else. "I'm looking forward to the tenth myself. Did you happen to bring the permission slip?"

Still gazing intently at her, he reached into his breast pocket and withdrew the paper she'd sent with the letter. "Now I've ascertained for myself that this is all legitimate, I'll sign it." He walked over to the receptionist's desk and wrote his signature in bold, decisive strokes, then handed her the form. "They're actually going to be on one of your television shows?"

Was he worried about Michael? "Yes. They'll each play a small part, but of course we'll rehearse before it's videotaped. Will that be a problem for Michael?"

His blue eyes were half-veiled. "I don't know. This is a situation he's never been in before. I'd hate for him to get sick right in the middle of your show."

"That's the beauty of taping rather than performing live. We could do a retake if anything like that happened," she hastened to assure him.

He looked pensive. "Come to think of it, he'll probably get sick the night before the visit. He has a history of getting too excited."

She swallowed hard. "Look, Dr. Wolfe. Please don't worry about it. If he's too sick to come to the studio on the tenth we'll reschedule it."

An expression of stunned surprise swept over his attractive face. "You're amazingly understanding."

She shook her head, the glossy black curls dancing about her face. "Not really. I've done a lot of tours of children's hospitals. Anything can happen at times like that, and usually does," she added with a sad smile.

"You came to Bremerton Memorial last Christmas, didn't you?"

"Yes. Were you there?" Surely she would have noticed him.

"I just missed you, but Michael saw you when you visited the children's wing on a publicity tour."

"Michael was among that group?" she cried out softly, oddly disturbed by a hint of criticism in his voice.

"Umm. I thought he had appendicitis but it turned out to be a severe stomach ache brought on by too much Christmas candy."

"Oh dear," Domini chuckled. "Do you work there?"

"Yes. I'm in pediatrics."

"My father was a family practitioner but ended up doing a lot of pediatrics himself."

He cocked his dark head to the side. "And where was that?" he asked, as if her statement mildly amused him.

"Tacoma. I used to help out in his office."

His eyes flickered. "You're full of surprises, Miss Loring. I'm relieved my children will be in such good hands. What time should I deliver them?"

"Ten o'clock," she answered quietly, aware that she was on trial in his eyes. Did he mistrust her on principle, or was it something personal? But how could that be? They'd never met before today.

"Barring complications, we'll be at the TV studio on time. I seriously doubt there'll be a problem, but I'll phone you immediately if there is."

"That's fine. Good night, Dr. Wolfe."

She followed him to the glass doors. He paused before leaving. "Do you need a lift someplace? I realize I've held you up after hours."

"That's kind of you but my car is out in the parking lot."

"Then I won't take up any more of your valuable time. Good night, Miss Loring. I'll see you on the tenth." His eyes swept over her once more, as if to memorize her body and her face, before he strode out of the building.

She stood rooted to the spot long after he'd disappeared. Domini had heard of instant physical attraction but had always discounted it until now. What an irony that the chemistry between them set off such negative sparks. He didn't like her, yet she knew intuitively that she disturbed him as much as he disturbed her. Nothing like this had ever happened to her before. She didn't have the slightest idea how to deal with the emotions he'd brought to life in her. It wasn't as if he were a mere stranger she'd never meet again.

He would be coming to the studio with his two boys in another week. She took a deep breath. The only thing she could do at this point was push all thoughts of Dr. Wolfe to the back of her mind and hope that her reaction to him was a passing aberration. When she saw him again, she'd realize that she'd only imagined his compelling attraction.

Domini gave herself a talking-to all the way to rehearsal but somehow she remained unconvinced, and that was what worried her.

CHAPTER TWO

DOMINI SCANNED the high cloud cover, confident and grateful that it wouldn't rain. A large crowd had already gathered in front of the TV studio to await the arrival of the Wolfe children. A welcoming banner with their names printed on it hung over the main doors for everyone to see. Dressed in full costume with her wig and crown, Domini sat on the throne used for her television program. It had been situated beneath a canopy near the curb. A gold carpet extended from the platform, down the steps and out to the street.

The presence of police, members of the press and a cameraman preparing to videotape the proceedings from start to finish heightened the excitement as dozens of children pressed forward wanting Domini's autograph.

She obliged as many as she could until Carter signaled the approach of a black Mercedes, which drove up to the curb. The police moved the crowd back to make way for the new arrivals. The brand of car banished once and for all Domini's preconceived image of an impoverished father struggling to keep up with astronomical medical bills.

The second she caught sight of his brown hair and strong profile her heart started to pound. During the past week Dr. Wolfe had been in her thoughts more than she cared to admit. Knowing she would see him again had only increased her tension. With her gaze fastened helplessly on him, she didn't notice the tow-headed little boy who suddenly scrambled from the back seat of the car toward her until he was practically upon her.

"Mike!" she heard Dr. Wolfe call, but the child seemed intent on reaching Domini.

She rose quickly to her feet and arranged her white tulle gown, which provided little protection against the brisk November cold. Slowly and carefully she descended the stairs to greet him. The crowd burst into spontaneous applause as the child flung his arms around Domini's slender waist, hugging her for dear life.

"Story Princess!" he gasped in a tone so full of emotion Domini felt a lump form in her throat as she hugged him back. Out of the corner of her eye she watched the approach of his father and straightened to welcome him. She had thought blue was his best color, but today he wore a fawn-colored suit with a cinnamon tie, and he looked devastatingly attractive.

"Dr. Wolfe," she greeted him in even tones.

"There's no question about your identity this morning," he murmured. His brilliant blue gaze fused with hers before traveling from the crystal crown atop her waist-long white-gold wig, over her curves, practically concealed by the floor-length jeweled cloak, and finally to her crystal shoes. With one sweep of his eyes she felt her body inflame and knew color filled her cheeks.

Quickly she concentrated on Michael, who still held on to her. His head tipped back and she smiled down into the brightest sky-blue eyes she'd ever seen. They were round as saucers, set in a smiling, gamin face with a smattering of freckles.

Domini searched for signs of illness, but he seemed perfectly normal and spry and she dismissed the notion that he might need a wheelchair or special help. He obviously had a problem that wasn't immediately visible.

"Am I really going to spend the whole day with you?" he asked, his heart in his eyes. His hand crept into hers, and clutched tightly.

"If that's what you'd like," she answered in a tremulous voice, praying that she could push his condition to the back of her mind and enjoy their time together.

"I wish you were my mom. You're beautiful!"

For a moment her head reeled. She didn't dare look at Dr. Wolfe but sensed that Michael's comment did not please him. Now was not the time for him to be reminded of the woman he'd married and lost. Wordlessly, Domini squeezed Michael's hand and extended her other hand to his brother. She noticed that the older boy's hair was a darker blond, though he shared the same facial features, without the roundness of early childhood. "Peter? I've been anxious to meet the author of that wonderful entry."

"Thanks for choosing my letter, Story Princess," he said politely, shaking her hand. Both boys were dressed in dark pants, shirts and sweaters of royal blue plaid, the same hue as their eyes, which stared at Domini in awe. "You're even prettier than you look on TV," Peter muttered.

"Are those Cinderella's shoes?" Michael asked, pointing at her feet.

"No, darling." She laughed softly, feeling her eyes smart and fighting for control. Tears would ruin her makeup and destroy the fantasy she'd determined to live for Michael's sake.

"Where's your magic wand?" he asked with such earnestness that everyone laughed, including the cameraman. Domini couldn't stop herself from glancing at Dr. Wolfe. But instead of a smile, she surprised a puzzled, almost sober expression on his lean face.

"I left it inside so I could greet you properly," she improvised, still trapped by Dr. Wolfe's intent regard. "Are you planning to stay for the day?" she asked him in an aside, strangely unsettled by his mood.

"I don't think so. This is their special moment. I'll be back for the children at five. Peter knows the number of the pediatrics clinic where I can be reached here in Seattle in case you need me. In any event, you have my number on the permission slip I signed."

"You have a clinic here as well as in Bremerton?"

"That's right. Three days out of every fourteen, I keep office hours in Seattle."

"That must mean a lot of commuting," she remarked.

"The ferry ride's about an hour long; it gives me a chance to relax."

She bit her lip. "Are there any special instructions concerning Michael?"

His brows formed the hint of a frown. "If he gets too tired or unmanageable, call me immediately."

"I won't get tired," Michael protested loudly, beseeching Domini to believe him.

She turned to his father and they exchanged a long, knowing look. "I think we won't worry about anything but your having a lovely time," Domini said gently, anxious to smooth over any tense moments. The last thing she wanted to do was upset him.

"Then I'll be off," their father announced. He knelt and put an arm around Michael, who still clung to Domini's hand. "Do everything the Story Princess tells you." Then he stood and patted Peter's shoulder. "Pete, look after your brother."

"He doesn't need to look after me. I'll be perfect!" Michael stated with such dignity that the crowd laughed again, but his father wasn't smiling.

"Dr. Wolfe," she whispered, worried by his concerned expression, "I promise to take the greatest care of your children."

There was an ominous pause. "I have no doubt of it, but please—let Michael know before the day is over that this is only make-believe." On that cryptic note he headed toward his car.

"Are we really going to be on TV tonight?" Michael questioned, drawing her attention away from the dark-haired man who got into the Mercedes and drove off.

"Yes. Your visit is going to be a special feature on the ten o'clock news." She turned toward the studio and reached for Peter's hand, which slipped eagerly into hers. "Try to forget the man with the camera. He's going to take pictures of us all day long and make a movie, which I'll send to you for a souvenir as soon as it's edited."

"Goody." Michael jumped up and down. "Then Daddy can see how much you *really* love us."

With a smile Domini ushered the boys in the direction of the building. "That's right. You'll have a movie to show all your friends and relatives." She wasn't surprised when they exchanged a private grin and mouthed the words, "Especially Dad."

"Are we going to do 'The Gingerbread Man' for your TV show?" Michael wanted to know as they entered the studio.

Peter shook his head, cautioning his brother to be quiet. Domini put her hand under Michael's round chin. "That's one of my favorite stories, too, but I thought you might like to wear costumes and enact a tale that hardly anyone has ever heard before."

Peter cocked his head to the side. "Really? How come?"

"Well, it's an old Russian fairy tale, and very few people in this country know about it. I've been waiting a long time to do this story, and now that I've met you, I think you'll both be perfect for the parts."

Michael looked as if she'd just handed him the world. "Are we going to do it right now?"

She placed her hands on the boys' shoulders and urged them forward. "I thought we'd take a tour of the studio first, then eat a catered lunch while I tell you the story of *The Little Blind Prince*. If you like it as much as I do, we'll let you choose parts and rehearse a couple of times before we tape it this afternoon."

Michael suddenly burrowed into her, clasping her tightly. "I love you, Story Princess. I want to live with you forever." Peter's expression seemed to echo his.

If it hadn't been for her long wig and crown and her elaborate costume, she would have swept him up in her arms. A pain wrenched her heart when she considered that Michael's days were numbered. Both boys had a sweetness that touched her deeply, even on such short acquaintance. "Why don't we pretend that today *is* forever." She tousled his fair hair before remembering that their father had counseled her to make sure Michael understood everything was make-believe. Already she'd disobeyed his final instructions, but she just couldn't help it.

"After we finish the taping, I'm taking you to an exciting place for an early dinner, where we'll meet a group of other children and a very good friend of mine, who's going to entertain all of us."

Again she caught a quiet message of happiness that passed between the two brothers. She sensed they were unusually close, no doubt because Peter knew the truth. Did Michael have any idea what the future held? she wondered. Their father's pain must be unbearable.

"Story Princess?" Peter whispered to Domini, forcing her to lean toward him. "Dad said we should go to the bathroom before we did anything else so we wouldn't interrupt your plans later on."

She couldn't help smiling. "Of course. It's straight down the hall on the left. I'll be waiting right here in my office."

Peter took hold of Michael's hand and pulled him along, but Michael kept looking at Domini. "You promise you won't disappear like you do on TV?"

"I promise. Cross my heart."

"Don't let that man with the camera come with us."

"Don't worry," she assured him with laughter in her voice.

"Did you really mean it? Will we really do speaking parts on the show?" Michael persisted despite Peter's frown.

Domini nodded. "You'd like that, wouldn't you?"

"Oh, yes. But Daddy said we'd be lucky to be stuck in the chorus section." His imitation of his father was brilliant.

She smothered a laugh. "There's no chorus in *The Little Blind Prince*. Only a little prince who's lame and blind and a magnificent blue fox."

"What's lame?"

"Mike!" Peter said in exasperation, exactly as their father had earlier. "Come on." He tugged at his brother's hand, forcing Michael to accompany him the rest of the way."

"We'll be right back!" Michael's voice floated down the corridor. By this time, most of the staff had congregated in the hallway, obviously as charmed by the Wolfe children as Domini was. She and her boss, Carter Phillips, exchanged a long look that spoke volumes.

"Still think the contest was a bad idea, Dom?"

"No," she answered in a husky voice. "But I hadn't counted on caring so much. The children are adorable. And M-Michael..."

"Seattle's answer to Shirley Temple. I know." Carter grinned. "He seems to be feeling quite chipper."

"Yes, but that's what's worrying me. How long can all that energy last?"

Carter fingered his mustache. "Probably as long as he's with you. I hope the camera caught that smile he flashed you on the pavement. It was as if he'd been confronted with all his Christmases and birthdays at once. He radiated joy. It was a sight I'll never forget."

And Domini would never forget his words: *I wish you were my mom. I want to live with you forever.*

As soon as the boys came back to her office, she began their tour. Then they headed for the studio to rehearse and tape the dramatized story, which went even better than expected. The boys acted their simple roles with touching sincerity, improvising lines based on Domini's explanations of the characters' actions. After that, they were allowed to look through the cameras and visit the control room. Before she knew it, it was four o'clock and time to go to the Space Needle Restaurant for their early dinner, followed by a magic show.

Carter had reserved a section of the famous revolving restaurant for that day, and some of the other children who'd written letters had been invited to join in the festivities. The Wolfe children, of course, would sit with Domini at the head table.

When the meal and the magic performance had ended, the two boys, along with the other children, ran to the windows to look out over the city of Seattle. "Can you see where we live, Pete?" Domini stood between them with her hands on their shoulders, amazed that Michael appeared to be holding up so well.

"Not yet, but we're coming around to it," Peter said.

Michael looked up at Domini. "Where do you live? Is it far away?"

"Even I'd like the answer to that question," a familiar male voice said behind Domini, causing all the children to whirl around.

"Dad!" the Wolfe boys squealed, running over to him. He gathered Michael up in one arm and put the other around Peter.

Every time Domini saw Dr. Wolfe her heartbeat quickened. She hadn't expected him to join them at this juncture but didn't blame him for wanting to check on Michael's condition. His presence unsettled her, but since both boys immediately started giving him a full account of their activities, she thought herself safe from his scrutiny as he listened patiently to their animated chatter.

"Well," he finally said, "I wouldn't be at all surprised if you've worn out the poor Story Princess. I've got an idea it's been a long day for everyone," he muttered, eyeing all the children, "and I imagine she's ready to go home, too." His incredible blue eyes suddenly fastened on hers, holding her spellbound. "Speaking of home, you were about to point it out to us."

She cleared her throat and turned back to the glass. "It's there on Mercer Island."

Michael's eyes grew round. "You live on Mercer Island? That's not very far, is it, Daddy? We can come visit you all the time."

An expressionless mask slipped over his father's face. "The Story Princess is a very busy person, Mike. If all the children who wanted to see her had their wish, she wouldn't have time to make records or be on television. Now—"

"She promised we could come and see her the next time we came to Seattle," Peter asserted quietly, staring soberly up at his father. Domini felt the tension emanating from the man and realized she'd said the wrong thing to his children. Although she couldn't understand it, she sensed that Dr. Wolfe wanted this day over, with no repeats. Maybe it had created too much excitement for Michael and would bring on complications.... Domini had no way of knowing, but her spirit plummeted. The day had been so perfect, she didn't want anything to mar it now.

"I think we won't worry about that right now," he said, and she could hear the hint of steel in his voice. "Thank the Story Princess for a wonderful time and we'll leave."

Michael started to cry. With tears spilling down his flushed cheeks he wriggled out of his father's arms and ran to Domini, burrowing himself against her. "This was the best day of my whole life," he blurted out, clutching the net of her gown with his small hands.

"Mine, too," Peter piped up. His blue eyes also had a telltale sheen.

It was up to Domini to avert disaster. Sucking in her breath, she put on her brightest smile. "Guess what? It's not over yet."

"It's not?" they cried in unison. She even managed to provoke a look of astonishment from their father.

"You won the contest, didn't you?" She smiled at each one of them as they nodded. "Well—you won some prizes, and if your father will drive you back to the TV studio, I'll have some of my helpers bring them out to your car."

"Goody!" Michael clapped his hands enthusiastically while Peter beamed. "Will you come with us? In our car?" Michael pleaded.

"I can't, Michael."

"Is it because your dress takes up too much room?"

Domini laughed gently, not daring to look at their father, who'd remained pointedly silent. "That's right."

"Thank you for everything you've done. I'm sure this is a day the boys will remember all their lives," Dr. Wolfe interjected on a sincere note. "Goodbye, Story Princess." He took hold of his children's hands and started walking toward the exit.

"Goodbye," the children called over their shoulders. "We'll be seeing you soon," they persisted in saying.

"Don't forget to watch yourselves on TV tonight at ten, if you can stay awake. Otherwise maybe your dad can tape it for you." The reminder caused a flurry of excitement as they disappeared through the doors, taking her heart with them. Would Michael still be alive if she ever did see them again? Poor Dr. Wolfe. To lose Michael would be utterly unbearable. If she could love him this much on first acquaintance, how much more would a parent feel? And Peter...

With a sorrow too deep for tears, Domini went back to the studio via a private entrance, changed into her street clothes and drove home. Under other circumstances she would have been on hand while their gifts were placed in the car. But this was no ordinary situation and Dr. Wolfe wouldn't thank her for creating additional problems. His manner bordered on hostility as it was. *But why?*

After a cup of tea and a hot shower, Domini put on her nightgown and relaxed on the couch in front of the TV for a few hours, awaiting the news. The screen became a blur as soon as she saw the boys' faces and heard their voices. It was too much. She got up, turned off the set and went to bed with a book, a new mystery she'd been looking forward to enjoying. After reading the first page for the hundredth time, she tossed the book onto the bedside table and willed sleep to come.

Carter had given her the following day off, assuming she needed a rest after her busy session with the boys. But the next morning, Domini found she couldn't bear her own company a minute longer and dressed casually for work. With nothing scheduled at the office, she could clean out files and do a little research on a story she wanted to narrate. Work would at least distract her from thoughts of the children—and Dr. Wolfe. Effortlessly, perhaps unintentionally, he created an excitement in her, an odd feeling of unrest. One moment, she wished she'd never met him, the next she yearned to see him again.

"Domini? I know this is really your day off, but I have a problem."

"That's okay, Marge." Domini stopped typing and looked up at the receptionist. "How can I help?"

"A man came in a minute ago and he insists on speaking to the person in charge. Carter's not here, but the man said he won't go away until he gets satisfaction."

"Did you tell him no one's available? To make an appointment with Carter for next week?"

"Of course, but he got me to admit the Story Princess was in the building before I figured out what he wanted, and he said he'd wait till hell froze over if necessary in order to talk to you."

"What a charming man," Domini murmured. "By all means, show the gentleman inside, Marge. He didn't give you any hint of what this is all about?"

She shook her head. "To be honest, I didn't dare ask him. He's gorgeous but scary, if you know what I mean."

Marge thought a lot of men were gorgeous so Domini didn't put much stock in the observation. Yet she couldn't quite shake off a sudden sense of foreboding that she wouldn't allow the other woman to see. "Why do people always come at the end of the day when we're ready to go home? Oh well, go ahead and send him in."

"Thanks." Marge sighed her relief and hurried out of the office. Within seconds Domini heard footsteps approach and looked up from the script she was editing. A pair of angry blue eyes pierced hers, and sent her into shock. Slowly she got to her feet, smoothing her beige sweater over her hips.

"Dr. Wolfe! Why didn't you tell Marge who you were?"

"And if I had, would you still be here, I wonder?"

She nervously smoothed a silky black lock of hair from her cheek. "Something's obviously wrong. What is it?"

His shrewd eyes studied her movements. "I think you know exactly why I'm here, Miss Loring."

At a total loss for words, Domini sank down in her chair. "Please...have a seat." She indicated one of the chairs opposite her but to her consternation he remained standing directly in front of the desk, his strong legs slightly apart. He wore another expensively tailored suit, of soft pearl gray this time, which accentuated his lean, masculine build. She cleared her throat. "When you left the restaurant with the children, I was under the assumption that everything was all right."

"Nothing's been all right since the boys won that contest!" His eyes practically bored through her. "A colleague of mine at the hospital fell all over himself commiserating with my *pain* this morning."

Domini straightened, placing her hands on the desk. "I can understand that. Everyone here shares your grief, Dr. Wolfe." Her voice sounded unsteady, despite her effort to control it.

"That's very interesting," came the mocking retort, "considering the fact that I'm not grieving, nor am I in pain. Since I didn't have the slightest inkling of what my colleague was talking about, my conversation with Dr. Gittens left us both somewhat confused. All thanks to you, *Miss Loring*."

Color spilled into her cheeks. "I'd say that if this is your reaction to something that brought your boys a little happiness, then you have a big problem, *Dr. Wolfe*."

"My sons played right into your clever hands. Tell me—out of all the thousands of letters you must have received, why did *my* children have the misfortune of being exploited for your latest publicity stunt?"

"Exploited?" His unconcealed anger and contempt stunned her.

"What else would you call it? And don't bother practicing your theatrics on me. You're not playing to an audience now. I'm immune to your kind."

Her chest heaved as she struggled to find the right words. "And what kind is that?" It was all she could do not to blurt out everything Peter had repeated in his letter.

"You'd do anything, say anything, to keep your face and name before the public. Do you want me to continue?"

His gaze swept over her in another scrutiny, one that was blatantly insulting. She swallowed hard and folded her arms as if to protect herself. "Look, Dr. Wolfe. I've seen what bitterness can do to people, but what you're transmitting to your sons is tantamount to a tragedy. Are you aware that Peter has picked up on your negative feelings? He's an eight-year-old boy, for heaven's sake. It's bad enough that he lost his mother, but—"

"Leave his mother out of it!" he demanded, raking an unsteady hand through the dark brown hair that just brushed the edge of his collar. "We were talking about your need to be constantly in the limelight. You and your company would make up any lie, use any excuse to accomplish your objective of making more money. And innocent children are your pawns."

She shook her head in exasperation. "What lie?"

He gripped the edge of her desk and leaned over so their faces were mere inches apart. "The game is up. There's no need to play the innocent any longer. All you have to do is issue a retraction, and we can both get on with our lives and pretend this experience was simply a bad dream."

Domini's brows furrowed; her annoyance conflicted with sympathy at his obvious distress. "I'm sorry, but I don't have the faintest idea what you're talking about."

"My *dying* child, Miss Loring."

Tears immediately sprang to her eyes. "Michael's a wonderful boy," she said haltingly. "I'd give anything to be able to make him well. Anything."

His harsh laugh rang out, startling her. "You're so far gone you actually believe your own fabrications. It's incredible. We can only hope the station manager will admit culpability and take the necessary steps.

Otherwise you'll be involved in a lawsuit—and some very undesirable publicity. Not even your beauty will save you then." Grabbing his coat, he wheeled around and started for the door.

"Dr. Wolfe!"

He checked his stride, glancing back at her in that arrogant, superior manner he'd displayed almost from the first.

"We're talking at cross-purposes. What monstrous crime have my employers and I supposedly committed? If this is a matter for an attorney, I'd like to know exactly what we're up against?"

He took a menacing step forward. "You demand your pound of flesh, don't you?" A nerve jumped at the side of his jaw. "Maybe this will explain." He reached in his topcoat and pulled a folded newspaper from the side pocket. "You do read the newspapers...."

"Of course," she answered in a quiet voice.

"Then this article might interest you." He handed her the morning edition of a major Seattle paper. On the top half of the front page was a large picture of her with her arms around Peter and Michael. The caption read, "Story Princess grants wish to dying child."

Domini gazed up at Dr. Wolfe, trying to understand him. Perhaps the word *dying* was simply too much for him, and in his grief, he was striking out at everyone. She lowered her head and finished reading the article. "Miracles still happen, this time to a family plagued by tragedy."

Domini's breath caught. "Pictured above with Seattle's own Story Princess are Michael and Peter Wolfe, sons of prominent physician, Dr. Jarod Wolfe, and the late Amanda Carlson, news reporter and personality for KLPC. Those in the Puget Sound area will recall the helicopter crash that took her life, leaving a grief-stricken family behind. Recently, tragedy has struck them again, but it is hoped that Michael's visit to his beloved Story Princess brought some needed magic into his life. Congratulations to the Wolfe children, who have speaking parts in the next episode of the Story Princess television program.''

Slowly, Domini put down the paper. *Amanda Carlson was his wife?* Domini remembered the tall, blond athletic-looking woman, but they'd never met. The knowledge that Dr. Wolfe had been in love with her pierced Domini with an unexpected shaft of pain. She thought she understood his anger now. He was still mourning his wife's death, on top of everything else.

"I-I'm sorry the media dredged up something so painful when you have Michael's illness to deal with." She didn't know what else to say.

"*What* illness?" he bit out. "The one *you* manufactured?"

"Manufactured?" she cried softly. "I don't know what—"

"Come off it, Miss Loring. My son is *not dying*, as you know perfectly well. And God willing, he'll live long enough to bury me one day. But thanks to you and this company, every person in the state of Washington is under the impression that my son is about to slip away from life.

"His picture is on the front page of the paper and my family's life is suddenly open to public speculation and conjecture. Your latest publicity campaign has interfered with our private lives and there'll be hell to pay as a result!''

CHAPTER THREE

"ARE YOU TELLING me the truth?" A great wave of joy brought Domini to her feet. "You mean Michael isn't ill? He's not going to die?"

His features looked chiseled out of stone. "You deserve an Academy Award."

"But Dr. Wolfe—you don't understand," she continued excitedly. "Peter said that Michael would be going to heaven soon and—"

A dark flush stained his cheeks. "Don't even try to blame this blatant lie on my son. Face the facts. Your company concocted this farce to wring every drop of emotion from your adoring fans, but I'm going to expose you unless you go to the media with a full confession. You can tell *that* to your boss."

Domini anticipated his next move and hurried around the end of her desk to prevent him from leaving. "I think you'd better read Peter's letter before you go," she said, out of breath. She'd backed up against the closed door in the ridiculous hope of blocking his exit.

At first she thought he was in too great a rage to hear her out. But something in her voice or expression must have reached him, because he stood motionless in the center of her office, his face noticeably pale. "May I see it?" he finally asked in a gravelly tone of voice.

Expelling a sigh, Domini moved away from the door and walked over to the file cabinet. Opening the middle drawer, she pulled out the Wolfe folder. Then she plucked the letter with its attached original envelope from the file and handed it to him, almost dreading the moment when he would discover the truth for himself.

She realized now that Peter had lied about Michael's condition. This was borne out as she watched their father's mouth tighten, his pallor grow more pronounced. Suddenly he looked up and his haunted expression shook her. "Dear Lord," he groaned, shaking his dark head. "I had no idea...."

Taking a deep breath, she said, "Under the circumstances, I'll talk to Carter about printing a retraction in the newspaper, as well as making a statement on television." He nodded in a daze. She bit her lip. "There must be a perfectly good explanation for what he did. Please don't tell Peter you saw his letter," she urged gently.

Deep grooves bracketed his taut lips. "You're asking the impossible, particularly after the unforgivable way I've attacked *you*." She heard him groan again as he read the letter a second time. "I should have figured it out long before now," he muttered, almost to himself. "In that wig, you do bear a superficial resemblance to Amanda. She had shoulder-length blond hair and a cultured speaking voice.

"The reference to his mother explains a great deal about why Peter went to the lengths he did. I haven't encouraged him to talk about his mother and that's where I've made a big mistake."

Domini rubbed her palms along her hips in an unconscious gesture, inexplicably disturbed by his explanation. "Does Michael remember her at all?"

"No." The curt reply made her wish she hadn't asked the question. "She died when he was four months old."

Domini knew that some women resumed their careers very soon after their babies were born, but she'd never been comfortable with that idea. If she ever did marry and have children, she hoped to stay home with them as much as possible. "Forgive me for mentioning it, Dr. Wolfe."

"There's nothing to forgive. It's life." His voice held no trace of animosity, but it held no animation, either. The bleak look in his eyes told its own story. Amanda Carlson's sons had inherited her Scandinavian coloring. Domini felt a curious envy for this woman, who'd been married to such a strong, vitally attractive man and had two beautiful sons with him. Her death must have killed something inside Jarod Wolfe.

Evidently the pain of losing his wife had made him close up, unaware of Peter's grief and helpless to alleviate it. Domini couldn't help but wonder how it would feel to be loved like that. Domini's father had loved her mother in much the same way and had never really recovered after she died.

"Could I bring you some coffee?" she asked. But he was shrugging into his coat, her question apparently lost on him. The expression in his eyes was unreadable as he gave her back the letter.

"Rest assured I'll get the truth out of Peter without divulging that this meeting ever took place."

She put a hand to her throat nervously. "Is it really necessary to say anything at all? What good would it accomplish now?"

"It might help me to understand where I'm failing as a father to my children."

Domini grew instantly remorseful. "Aren't you being too hard on yourself? Peter's not the first child to tell a lie for reasons he thinks are perfectly understandable. He wants your respect and love more than anything in the world and thought that winning the contest would make you proud of him. Don't you see? He believes everything you say because he adores you."

He blinked. "That was quite a testimonial. Please don't misunderstand. I appreciate what you're trying to say but it doesn't excuse Peter's repeating all my comments verbatim to a total stranger, or lying about something—no matter how justified it seemed at the time. The sooner he and I have a little talk, the better. He needs to know that what he did has hurt everyone involved and caused me to say some unforgivable things to you. You have every right to tell me to go to hell."

"I admit I was tempted." She smiled in an attempt to humor him, but he had already reached the door.

"The fact that you didn't tells me a great deal about your character. Good night, Miss Loring." With a barely perceptible nod of his head, he left the office. Again, she experienced that intangible sense of loss— a ridiculous reaction, under the circumstances.

The sound of his footsteps receding down the corridor made the building seem tomblike to Domini. She leaned against the doorjamb, limp from their meeting. Her joy at learning that Michael was perfectly healthy turned her whole world around. But Peter's lie had resulted in unexpected consequences.

What made Peter do it? How would the confrontation with his father affect him? She had it in her heart to feel sorry for Dr. Wolfe because she knew he adored the boys. Peter's lie had obviously come as a stunning blow. She'd never forget the look on his face. It was clear that he couldn't conceive of Peter telling a lie, let alone one of such magnitude. Neither could Domini, for that matter. There was more to it than just wanting to win, she mused sadly.

Deep in thought, Domini shrugged into her coat and picked up her purse, unable to do any more work. Suddenly the idea of going home held no appeal. Her apartment was empty and uninviting. She didn't want to be alone tonight, even wished she hadn't turned down a date with one of the cameramen. Maybe she'd drive to Tacoma and spend the weekend with old friends in familiar surroundings. Returning to her childhood home might ease the turmoil created by one Dr. Wolfe. She needed to put all thoughts of him out of her mind. No other man had ever affected her like this, incensing her one minute, leaving her breathless with longing the next. And though she dreaded ever experiencing his anger again, she felt that her life had already been altered in some way by their encounters. The thought of never seeing him again was strangely depressing.

THE WEEKEND IN TACOMA turned out to be the tonic Domini needed. Three days had passed and the Wolfe affair no longer seemed so traumatic. She'd spent every waking hour with friends and had almost managed to put the entire episode out of her mind. Michael would live a normal life. That was all that really mattered.

As Domini entered the recording studio on a gust of freezing rain, Marge got up from her desk and hurried toward her. One look at the receptionist's distraught expression, and Domini felt every bit of calm she'd achieved in Tacoma vanish.

"Dr. Wolfe is here again," Marge whispered. "He's waiting in your office."

Domini's heart began to thud. "Is he upset?"

"I'd say so. He's been trying to reach you all weekend and left several messages on the answering machine. He was standing outside the doors when I arrived for work this morning. What's going on?"

Domini unbelted her coat and slipped out of it. "It's a long, complicated story. I'll tell you about it later."

"Holler if you need help."

"Thanks, Marge," she murmured absently, unable to control the excitement welling up inside despite her attempts to quell it. She scarcely noticed the other staff who'd arrived for work, and entered her office slightly flushed and out of breath. Why was Dr. Wolfe seeking her out again? It made no sense at all.

"Finally," his deep voice grated. He'd evidently been studying the wall chart outlining her hectic schedule.

She whirled around, startled by his comment. As his penetrating blue eyes assessed her in one sweeping glance, she felt momentarily thankful that she'd dressed more formally than usual for work this morning in her favorite plum suede suit. "Why do you say 'finally' when I'm early?" He still had on his tan overcoat and he looked magnificent—there was no other word for it. She avoided his searching gaze and sat down at her desk.

As on Friday, he remained standing. "Because I've been phoning your home on Mercer Island all weekend to no avail."

She raised her eyebrows slightly. "I've been in Tacoma with friends. How did you get my number?"

"I have my sources." He slid one hand inside his coat pocket. "Does that annoy you?"

"No," she blurted out. "I'm just surprised, because it's unlisted."

"I can understand why. There are times when I wish mine was," he said wryly, "but then I wouldn't have any business."

Domini chuckled. "My father used to say the same thing. He had a rule that I could only talk on the phone to my friends for two minutes at a time, for fear a patient wouldn't be able to get through."

The first smile she'd seen broke out on his handsome face. "I'll have to remember that when Michael and Peter reach the impossible teens. Which brings me to the reason why I'm here." In an uncharacteristically hesitant manner, he ran both hands through his hair. "I need to apologize properly. It's obvious I don't know my own son as well as I thought I did. I certainly had no right to charge into your office on Friday and threaten you. That was unforgivable of me."

Her hands gripped the arms of the chair. "Not unforgivable," she said in a husky voice after a short interval of silence. "I'm not so sure I wouldn't have done the same thing in your place, given the same circumstances. The lie *did* receive local coverage and you were the last person to know. I'm sorry."

"I don't deserve to be let off lightly." He grimaced. "I don't know how you put up with me on Friday."

"I don't, either." But an impish grin belied her statement.

"That makes me feel a little better." He smiled slightly and a faint gleam entered his beautiful eyes. "Tell me something," he added more soberly. "There must have been other letters besides Peter's that mentioned illness. Was it because of Amanda that you chose my son's letter in the end?"

The genuine appeal in his question puzzled her. "Why would she have anything to do with my decision?"

He folded his arms across his broad chest. "Either you're a superb actress or you really didn't know."

Just when she'd started enjoying their apparent friendliness, he'd come out with some nebulous hostility that kept the conflict alive.

He scrutinized her with deliberation. "It occurred to me that you might have chosen Peter's letter, knowing the press would capitalize on my wife's death in that helicopter crash. Even you would have to agree that after coverage like you saw in the newspaper, the Story Princess is going to be front and center in everyone's mind."

Domini rubbed her forehead where she could feel the beginning of a headache. "I swear to you I knew nothing about your wife. In fact, if I'd had any inkling of the relationship—particularly as we both worked for KLPC—I'd have been forced to choose another letter from someone with a totally unrelated background. I had no idea that Amanda Carlson used her maiden name here at the studio."

The very air seemed to vibrate with tension until he finally murmured, "I believe you."

Domini sighed deeply and closed her eyes. Obviously Peter's lie had brought the whole ugly nightmare of his wife's death to the surface again. "Did you have your talk with Peter?"

He nodded then sat down in one of the chairs, crossing an ankle over the opposite knee. "I asked him to tell me *exactly* what he put in his letter to you. When he couldn't look me in the eye, I waited and finally he burst into sobs and it all came out."

She leaned forward. "It must have helped a lot to know he felt remorse and could admit to his mistake."

"Peter has quite an advocate in you," he said, his voice full of some emotion she couldn't quite identify.

"He's a wonderful boy." She swallowed hard. "Did he tell you why he did it?"

His gaze locked with hers. "He did. He said he wanted to help Michael win the contest because Michael loved *you* so much. So he took my suggestion."

"What suggestion?"

He grimaced and rubbed the pad of his thumb along his lower lip. "I told him not to bother entering the contest because he'd be wasting his time, that a child would have to be on his deathbed in order to win."

Domini blinked. "You honestly believed that, didn't you?"

"Did and still do," he mocked. "You know I'm right." Unexpectedly he smiled and the warmth of his smile spread through her whole body.

She averted her head in an attempt to fight his potent charm. "I'll admit that knowing he would never get well influenced my decision to some degree, but there were many letters revealing problems as serious as Michael's."

He sat back propping both elbows on the arms of the chair. "Don't leave me hanging. What did Peter say that made the final difference?"

She flicked an imaginary piece of lint from the sleeve of her jacket. "I was afraid you'd ask that question."

A low laugh escaped him. "I'm in so deep now, I couldn't possibly climb out. Live dangerously and tell me."

An unknowingly seductive smile curved the corners of her mouth. "I think the reference to my being a grade-B actress probably did the trick, possibly helped by the line that I craved attention." She tried to say it without breaking into laughter but failed. Unfortunately he didn't seem to find it amusing. The animation left his face.

"I have no excuse for the things I said about you," he admitted, shaking his head. "None at all. And last but not least is my crime of ingratitude. I never did tell you that my children spent the most thrilling day of their lives with you last Thursday. I'd like to correct that oversight by taking you out for an evening as my way of saying thank-you. Are you free Wednesday night? I have tickets to *The Marriage of Figaro*. Please—don't turn me down."

Here Domini had been afraid he'd walk out of her life forever, and now she only had to make it to Wednesday night. Alive with excitement she got to her feet to give herself time to recover. She could scarcely believe he wanted to see her again. "I'd enjoy that very much."

"Good. Now if you'll give me your address, I'll pick you up at seven."

"I think it would be better if I met you at the opera house. We'll be recording late every night this week, but I'll be able to slip away around seven-thirty and take a taxi there."

A flash of irritation came and went in his eyes, so fast she wasn't sure she'd really seen it. "Then I'll look for you outside the box office before curtain."

"I'll be wearing a black-and-white print dress if that will help."

He gave her an intensely personal look. "You'd stand out in any crowd regardless of what you wore. I'll find you."

Domini had trouble settling down to work once he'd gone. She knew that reading any more into his invitation than a desire to make amends, was probably foolish. But like his children, he had charisma, and she found herself looking forward to spending the evening with him, particularly since he no longer blamed her or the studio for the contest results.

From the first she'd wished she'd met him under different circumstances. She was still under the spell of his lazy smile, still charmed by the way it had transformed his features. She wanted to see that smile again. In truth, she wanted to be the one responsible for it.

"WHERE WOULD YOU LIKE to eat?" Jarod wanted to know as they pulled into the traffic after the opera. "I'm prepared to indulge your slightest whim. After all, I'm escorting Seattle's greatest celebrity. Where does the in-crowd go these days?''

His reference to the in-crowd must have been prompted by memories of his wife. Domini's smile faded. ''I don't know about anyone else but I thought you might enjoy eating at a little bistro not far from here. Peter told me how much you love rich desserts while we were having a snack at the studio the other day. Jorgio's wife makes a fabulous cheesecake, as well as Hungarian goulash that's out of this world. It's the kind of place I thought you'd like.''

''Is this where the food is served by a gypsy with a big black mustache who plays the violin and pulls coins from little boys' ears?''

Domini nodded. ''The very one. He'll play an entire Vivaldi concerto if you ask him nicely, but he only does tricks for children. I promised the boys I'd take them there if they ever come to visit me again.''

His hands tightened on the steering wheel. ''I know. The children have talked of nothing else.''

''It's my favorite place in Seattle,'' she forged ahead, not wanting the slightest cloud to mar their evening. ''I could listen to the music all night. Jorgio was concertmaster of the Budapest chamber orchestra before he and Anna emigrated a few years ago. We've become good friends.''

''Then let's go there by all means.'' His voice was friendly and Domini decided she must have imagined his disapproving tone a few minutes earlier. She gave him directions to the restaurant, then neither spoke again until they arrived.

Her white cashmere coat protected her from the biting chill of the night air, but it wasn't responsible for the languorous warmth that stole through her body when she brushed against him as he ushered her from the car to the restaurant across the street.

"Delmonica!" Jorgio cried out his nickname for her as they entered the bistro. He kissed her on both cheeks before inspecting her escort. She made the introductions, then Jorgio showed them to a table in the corner and lit the candle that stood in the center of the crisp linen cloth.

"So," he said, his black eyes sparkling, "you are the father of the famous and talented Wolfe children I saw on television. I'm so sorry about the little boy."

Domini intercepted a speaking glance from Dr. Wolfe and turned to Jorgio. "I'm afraid there was a mistake, Jorgio, but a wonderful one. Michael is *not* ill, nor is he likely to be."

Jorgio blinked. "This certainly calls for a celebration. I will play whatever you wish, Dr. Wolfe. Simply name it!"

Domini looked across the table at Dr. Wolfe. The flame of the candle seemed to burn a hot blue in his eyes. The soft light emphasized the lines and angles of his handsome face, shadowing the slight cleft in his strong chin. His gaze moved slowly over Domini, and she felt her skin heat, as though she'd moved too close to the flame.

"I have a special love for Borodin," he said at last.

"Ah . . ." Jorgio nodded as if immensely pleased. "You are a genuine music lover. I know just the piece. Order your dinner, then I will come back and play for you. Conrad!" He snapped his fingers at one of the waiters. "Bring the best house wine for my guests."

The young black-haired man filled their wineglasses. As he hurried away, Domini took a sip, wondering if it was wise since she already felt intoxicated just being in the same room with Dr. Wolfe.

His eyes studied her moist red mouth. "The children tell me you sometimes sing in public. I wonder if I could coax you into singing here tonight with Jorgio accompanying you."

"Your children know entirely too much," she said with an impish smile, "but to be frank, I don't think you'll be ready for 'Tom Thumb's Ride' or 'Little Miss Henny Penny' after Borodin."

His mouth twitched at the corners. "I was thinking more along the lines of an aria from *Aida*. The friends to whom you introduced me at intermission said you could have sung the lead in tonight's performance."

She nodded reflectively. "There was a time when I thought I'd pursue an opera career, but it turned out to be my father's dream more than mine. Out of respect for his memory and all the encouragement he and Mother gave me, I occasionally sing for a special event."

"It isn't often that an opera singer's beauty measures up to her voice. You could have the whole world at your feet—not just the state of Washington."

Her hand tightened on the stem of her wineglass. "I have no interest in being a public figure, Dr. Wolfe. As for beauty, it's all relative and where singing is concerned, it's the voice that's important."

His eyes flickered mysteriously. "Why don't we agree to differ on that point?" To Domini's relief the waiter chose that moment to take their orders for dinner. When he went away again, Dr. Wolfe unexpectedly asked, "Isn't your own television show a fairly public way to earn a living?"

She took a deep breath. "I wasn't always the Story Princess. I started out doing the singing and narrations for children's records and tapes."

"I know. We have every tape you've ever made, but Michael plays 'The Gingerbread Man' constantly."

"That was my favorite story as a child. He's a boy after my own heart." She smiled wistfully.

"So from recording you catapulted into television," he continued.

"Very reluctantly," she corrected him, "and only on the condition that my image be changed to allow me a normal life away from the studio."

His eyes narrowed. "But your voice will always give you away. You sing divinely. I really do want to hear you sing for me sometime soon."

Her heart skipped a beat at the idea that there might be a next time. "Thank you. Maybe someday." The arrival of dinner prevented further conversation, because Jorgio produced his violin and in his flamboyant manner began to play a piercingly tender love song.

The combination of the music, the wine and the nearness of the exciting man seated across from her put Domini in a rare state of euphoria. "Tell me something honestly. Did you pick *The Marriage of Figaro* for my sake, or yours?" she asked him as soon as Jorgio had finished playing and moved to another table.

"Both. I rarely take time off without the children. When I do, this is the kind of evening I enjoy most."

"A doctor's life is a demanding one."

"Almost as demanding as yours."

His preoccupation with her work began to irritate her. "The boys tell me you do a lot of sailing."

A trace of a smile lingered on his lips. "I doubt either of us has any secrets left."

She smiled back. "Maybe one or two."

"What conclusions have you drawn?" His voice was casual, his eyes oddly intent. He wiped the corner of his mouth with a napkin.

"That you're devoted to your children and your practice. It can't be easy to balance your responsibilities, to find enough time for everything you have to do."

"Well, it's certainly not the way I envisioned life when I married Amanda."

"No," she muttered under her breath, not looking at him for fear she'd see that bleakness in his eyes again.

"Shall we go?" His question was purely rhetorical, since he'd already risen from the table. Obviously, talking about his wife had disturbed him. She stood up as he came around behind her, then he lightly took her arm. Jorgio saw them leaving and rushed over to say good-night. Jarod thanked him for the music and complimented him on the meal before they went out to the car.

"I'll drive you to the parking lot and follow you home," he said firmly.

"That's not necessary. It's a long drive and we live in opposite directions."

"I asked you out for the evening and I intend to see you home," he insisted on a tone of finality.

It started raining as they drove across the bridge to Mercer Island, his car close behind hers. By the time she pulled into the driveway in front of her building the downpour began in earnest. She'd scarcely had time to unclasp her seat belt when Jarod knocked on the passenger-side window. Domini undid the lock and he quickly slid in, shutting the door. His arm stretched along the back of her seat and brushed the collar of her coat. It was the merest touch but she felt electrified.

"Before you get away from me, I want to thank you for giving me the chance to apologize properly, Miss Loring. I've enjoyed this evening more than you know. You're a woman of many talents."

There it was again. The innuendo alongside the compliment, making her uneasy. "I have the feeling you didn't expect to enjoy the evening at all."

"I wouldn't put it quite that way. Let's just say you're not as predictable as I'd imagined, and I'm beginning to see why my boys are so enamored of a woman who for all intents and purposes is a total stranger to them."

Dr. Wolfe believed in being brutally honest, she realized. "I'd like to think your children and I became friends the other day, but it's obvious you don't approve of further contact. Even though I made a promise to them, I won't keep it under the circumstances. There must be no more lies or misunderstandings."

"Amen to that," he returned, idly fingering a black lock of hair curled against her neck. The slightest touch of his skin against hers sent prickles of awareness through her body. "But if I forbid them to see you again, I'm afraid they'll never forgive me for it."

Domini lifted cloudy green eyes to him, not understanding.

"You were the magic that made their day one of enchantment. You, and only you, accomplished something that not even I have been able to do since

their mother died. Their eyes were shining like stars
when I first walked in the house the day they got your
letter." His hand tightened in her hair but she was
positive he wasn't aware of it. "I resented you for
that."

Her breath caught. "Do you still resent me?"

"Maybe," he confessed huskily before letting go of
the silky tendrils curling around his fingers. She enjoyed the feel of his hand against her skin and wished
he hadn't removed it. "Peter wants to see you again
and explain himself. Apologize. Needless to say, Michael wants to be with you all the time. No, that isn't
exactly true. He wants to live with you forever."

Domini thought she understood. "He only says that
because I'm part of a fantasy he'll outgrow in another year." Some vulnerable part of him made her
want to reach out and comfort Jarod Wolfe. *Didn't he
know how much his boys loved him?*

He flashed her a speaking glance. "*We* know that,
but in the meantime, they've both made elaborate
plans for the next meeting, which includes the four of
us. I told the boys I'd drive them into Seattle next
Sunday so they could spend some time with you. If
you're free, we could take in the Aquarium—Peter's
idea—and go out for dinner somewhere along the
waterfront. According to Michael your favorite food
in the whole world is king salmon."

"That's true." She smiled in remembrance of their
conversation. She reminded herself that the invitation would never have been issued if it hadn't been for
his boys, and her smile slowly faded. "I'd really love
to spend time with Peter and Michael, but I'm leaving
town on Sunday. I'll be away for three weeks. Perhaps when I come back?"

He removed his arm abruptly from the back of the seat. She expected him to get out of the car, but he didn't. "You know enough about children of that age to realize that three weeks sounds like ten years. If it's all right with you, I'd like to set a date right now—to soften the blow."

"I'm afraid I can't because—"

"You don't need to explain," he cut her off. "I warned the children this would happen, that an outing wouldn't be possible. They can't comprehend the life of a celebrity."

"You didn't let me finish," Domini asserted, trying to keep the anger from her voice. "Carter has arranged a tour of a dozen department stores in the Puget Sound area. It's part of the studio's winter promotion. I'll be making personal appearances and autographing record jackets. Depending on the success of the tour, I might be gone longer than three weeks. But the minute I return to Seattle I'll call the boys and set up a date. You have my word on that."

He eyed her for a long moment before levering himself from the car and coming around to her side. He pulled open her door, and without saying anything, he walked her to the front door of her building.

"Thank you for a lovely evening," she said, taking the initiative. "Despite your misgivings, I'm looking forward to being with the children again. As I said, I'll call them as soon as I know my plans. Good night."

"Good night." An onlooker might have been convinced by his smile, but Domini could see that it didn't reach his eyes. He didn't believe she'd keep her promise. "May your tour be a huge success," he called over his shoulder.

Once inside her apartment, she leaned against the closed door with her head in her hands, unaware of the passage of time. The man was an enigma. He'd gone to great lengths to make sure the boys would see her again, yet he admitted that he resented her and intimated that he didn't trust her. So how could she have wanted to feel those mocking lips against hers? How could she have craved the touch of his hands in her hair?

CHAPTER FOUR

AFTER A RESTLESS NIGHT, Domini awakened early and hurried to the studio. Knowing she'd be away for three weeks, Carter had arranged for her to tape eight shows before she left Seattle. Because of her frequent absences, it was studio policy to tape the programs at least two months in advance. Even so, her first priority was to talk to Michael and Peter and reassure them of her intentions.

As luck would have it, the boys had left for school and the doctor was making rounds at the hospital, this according to Mrs. Maughan. Domini asked the housekeeper to tell the boys she'd called and to explain that she'd arrange a day with them in Seattle, as soon as she returned from her tour.

The woman good-naturedly promised to pass on the message and assured Domini the boys would be ecstatic. Domini replaced the receiver, aware of a sharp disappointment that she hadn't been able to speak to the children themselves—or to Dr. Wolfe. On the other hand, she didn't feel quite as guilty as their father had made her feel the night before.

At least now the boys had proof of her good intentions. And if it surprised Dr. Wolfe that she'd taken the time to call his children, then so much the better. For some unknown reason, he didn't approve of her, but she didn't know if it was because he classified her as a celebrity or because he harbored a particular grievance.

Confused and still a little hurt, Domini plunged into her work. She was preparing a series of new narrations and welcomed Carter's announcement that they'd be taping after hours every night until she left on tour. That way she'd be too exhausted to think. As it was, she jumped every time the phone rang, hoping to hear Jarod's deep voice, then chided herself for hoping.

By the end of the week Domini had worn herself out. On Friday night, she submitted, with less enthusiasm than usual, to the makeup artist, then got into the first of her various costumes. She had to open each show as the Story Princess in full costume and crown, then do a quick change into another costume to portray a role in a fairy tale, along with her fellow actors.

Though everyone involved at the studio was a seasoned professional, there was still a lot of time spent waiting while sets, lights and sound were checked by the floor director and the script assistant discussed a last-minute line change.

That night's taping would take longer than usual because they were enacting "The Twelve Dancing Princesses," and some of the ballerinas from a local ballet school were late in arriving. The girls were hurried into their costumes and makeup while the other cast members stood around the set.

The scene was slightly chaotic before the countdown and Domini's nerves were frazzled. The honey-blond wig she had to wear as the oldest princess tangled in the breeze when the fan was turned on to create illusion of wind. The director had to call in the hairdresser to spray her wig. It seemed they'd never start taping and Domini was fast losing her patience.

"You look good enough to eat," Allen said to her as he entered the studio dressed as her father, the king.

"Oh no, you don't," Paul chimed in, giving Domini a wink. "I'm the hero in this production, so leave her alone."

"Will you two please be quiet?" Domini begged. The overhead microphones, which had been turned on just minutes before, picked up the slightest little breath or cough. "You're embarrassing me."

"You shouldn't look so gorgeous, then," Allen persisted. "It's your own fault, you know."

"For heaven's sakes, let's get on with it!" Helen spoke up, sounding as tired as Domini felt. The four of them had worked together over a three-year period and enjoyed a unique camaraderie, but sometimes Allen overdid the teasing. He reminded her of her mother's brother, who joked his way through every family gathering.

"Domini?" She heard her name called over the sound system. It was Carter. As the show's executive producer, he generally came to watch how things were progressing. "Come into the control booth for a minute. There's someone who wants to see you before we start taping."

Curious, Domini made her way to the booth, then paled when she caught sight of Dr. Wolfe. He lounged against the wall, wearing a dark tailored suit and a crisp, immaculate shirt. His deep-blue eyes seemed to flare with an oddly fierce light as she approached him.

How long had he been watching Allen's ridiculous antics? she wondered.

"I hope you don't mind, Miss Loring," he murmured, then smiled, and she glimpsed a flash of white teeth more dazzling than his shirt.

"We had a chat in my office," Carter explained. "We've worked out a statement to give the press about Michael, and all is now well. Dr. Wolfe asked if he could see what actually goes on here at the studio so I told him to come along and watch a taping."

Domini's pulse was always erratic around Jarod Wolfe, but right now it had surged out of control. *What was his real reason for coming all the way over to the television studio?* "I'm afraid you'll wish you hadn't come. It's taking forever to get this under way tonight."

His eyes roved over her figure, unconcealed by the ivory gown and pale blue cape, before returning to her face. "Don't worry about me, Miss Loring. I'm fascinated, if you want to know the truth."

"You may not feel the same way after you've been here an hour. If you'd like, I'll ask one of the guys to take you to the projection room and you can watch the video of the children's visit. Then you can take it home for the boys."

"I'd prefer to watch you tape the show, then perhaps we could view the movie together. Unless you have other plans."

Her breath caught. "No, I have no plans for tonight."

"Then I'll wait for you."

"Well, now, with everything settled I can be off." Carter shook Dr. Wolfe's hand, bent to kiss Domini's made-up cheek and left the booth. "Be ready on Sunday by eleven," he called over his shoulder.

A pair of shrewd blue eyes took in the proceedings but gave nothing away. An onlooker wouldn't know that Carter's comings and goings were always punctuated with a kiss. It meant nothing, yet she had a disturbing impression that Dr. Wolfe was filing that kiss away to be used against her at some later time.

"I'll see you in a while, Dr. Wolfe." She felt his eyes on her as she left the booth and walked over to her place on the set. Though she'd memorized her part, she was thankful that the script assistant was standing by to prompt her in case she forgot a line. Anything was possible with Dr. Wolfe scrutinizing every movement, taking in every word. She'd never been this nervous performing in her whole life!

Once the taping had begun, Allen behaved like the professional he was, and everything went without a flaw, much to Domini's surprise and satisfaction. She took pride in her work and wanted Dr. Wolfe to be impressed with the expertise of the group. For some reason, she still felt as if she were under suspicion. She couldn't shake off the feeling that he found her wanting in some way she didn't understand.

He seemed to find her attractive, but occasionally she'd catch a strange glint in his eye, a veiled note of mockery or sarcasm in his voice, and her spirits would plummet.

Because everything went smoothly, the taping didn't take as long as she'd feared, and within forty-five minutes she sat in the projection room with Dr. Wolfe, minus her costume and makeup. For the moment they were alone. She ran a shaky hand through her black curls.

"Despite the fact that you look good enough to eat, as your colleague suggested earlier, it doesn't require a medical training to see you're dead on your feet. Why do you push so hard?''

So he *had* heard Allen clowning around! ''Normally I don't,'' she said, getting up to feed the videotape of the children's visit into the machine. ''Tell me something, Dr. Wolfe. When you know you're going to be gone from your practice for an extended period of time, don't you burn the candle at both ends in an effort to prepare for it?''

''Touché.'' He chuckled as she turned out the lights, then sat down again to watch the movie with him. But his laughter faded as the movie began and the sound of his voice reached their ears. The cameraman had caught everything, including Michael's escape from the car before his father could stop him.

Dr. Wolfe sat forward and gazed at the screen in fascination. Domini, too, felt a flutter of anticipation because she hadn't yet seen the video.

Michael's cherubic face lit up the screen as he threw himself into Domini's arms. The words, ''I wish you were my mom. You're beautiful!'' resounded in the dark intimacy of the room. The cameraman had captured that moment of special communion between her and Michael.

''Dear Lord,'' Jarod Wolfe's voice grated reverently.

Domini was thankful for the darkness because she couldn't stop the tears from spilling down her cheeks. Though she knew Michael was perfectly healthy, at that moment on the screen, she'd believed him to be deathly ill. She could still remember the feel of those arms clasping her waist.

Neither of them spoke as the movie revealed the joy of two children visiting a fairy-tale princess. A close-up of Peter as he portrayed the Blue Fox, costumed in an outfit made for a child his size, brought a familiar lump to Domini's throat.

"Don't weep, dear prince. I'll always take care of you. I will use my eyes to survey your kingdom. My ears will hear the words of your people. I love you, dear prince. Please don't be sad."

His performance could have moved a heart of stone. And Michael, dressed as the Little Blind Prince, gave a heartrending performance. He even remembered to drag his left leg during Domini's entire narration.

In an unexpected move, Dr. Wolfe rose to his feet and walked over to the machine to shut it off. They hadn't seen the part at the Space Needle yet, but perhaps the movie had become too much of an emotional experience for him to watch any more. She'd lost the battle with tears and could just imagine how the images of his sons, so innocent in their delight, must have affected him.

"I don't think there are words to describe my feelings right now. All I can do is thank you for this gift, which I know the family will treasure all our lives. The boys will be absolutely thrilled when they see this!"

Domini got up and turned on the light, tired but happy for the first time since she'd met him. Their eyes met across the room. "When Carter first approached me about the contest, I was hesitant. I'm against contests in principle, but getting to know your children was a privilege. I want you to know I tried to call the boys the other day—to assure them that we'll get together soon."

He frowned, his manner suddenly wary. "One reason I decided to drop by the studio tonight was to talk to you about that."

Something in his tone caused her to stiffen. "Did I do the wrong thing?"

"Not if you meant it."

"And you don't think I did, obviously. How dare you make a presumption like that when you don't even know me?"

He frowned again and his features darkened. "I dare because it's Peter I'm concerned about here. He feels a deep need to beg your forgiveness. He understands that what he did was wrong, and now he's almost made himself ill over it. Until he faces you, I doubt that life around our house will ever be the same.

"Now he's waiting for your call, which may or may not come."

Domini started to say something in her own defense, but he wasn't listening. "I recognize that you have no obligation to my children, Miss Loring. I know you mean well, but something else will come up, preventing you from keeping your promise to them. You told me yourself you have no idea when your tour will end. I think it would have been better if you hadn't made that phone call. It raised Peter's hopes. I don't want them dashed."

"Do you honestly think I'd do that to the children?" Her voice shook with emotion.

He pulled the tape from the machine and moved toward the door. "I don't doubt that you believe what you say. However, I have some concern about your ability to follow through. You have a demanding career. Your work, which you do better than anyone else I can possibly imagine, will always come first with you. But Peter doesn't understand that." He paused. "Good luck on the tour. And thank you for this." With video in hand he left the projection booth.

She stood there, immobilized by too many emotions. Peter's letter came vividly to mind. "My dad says...you don't care about children. All you crave is attention." Their dinner out had been a token gesture, after all.

On the way home, she mulled over Dr. Wolfe's parting words. The man was impossible. He'd warned her not to come near him or his children unless she could deliver on her promise. Right now she couldn't contemplate ever talking to him again, much less facing him. Not even for Peter's sake.

The following day she put her apartment in order and began packing. Her neighbor promised to come in every few days to collect the mail and water the plants. Fortunately Domini didn't have to take a lot of clothes with her, since she wore the Story Princess costume for every appearance. The rest of the time, when she wasn't working, she could dress casually as she explored the little side streets and visited nearby towns. A bookworm like her father, she adored browsing in old bookstores, looking for out-of-print copies of tales she might be able to use in her narrations.

Carter picked her up on Sunday morning and drove her to Bellingham, where she would make her first public appearance of the tour in a newly built complex. They talked business during the first part of the trip. But when Carter started to ask questions about Dr. Wolfe, Domini changed the subject and he was astute enough to let the matter drop. Instead, she asked him about his son, Sean, and effectively turned the conversation away from herself.

Children's Playhouse security man, Bill Harris, met them at the hotel when they arrived. Carter had hired him to drive Domini from city to city and act as her personal bodyguard during tours, a precaution that suited her perfectly well. She sighed with relief when Carter told her he had to return to Seattle immediately. She didn't feel up to discussing the possibility of traveling to Spokane to do another Story Princess tour. The contest and its aftermath had completely drained her.

Right now she needed the peace and support she derived from the soft-spoken Bill. The retired police officer reminded her of her father in some ways and was just the person to keep her mind off Dr. Wolfe and their last devastating encounter.

A week into the tour Domini came down with a head cold. At first she ignored it, but after a couple of days she grew hoarse and went to bed at Bill's urgings. All further appearances had to be canceled.

She phoned Carter from her hotel room, apprising him of the situation. He told her to take a week off to recuperate, to pamper herself. When she recovered, they'd discuss Spokane. She couldn't imagine doing another tour the way she felt right now but didn't express her feelings to Carter, except to thank him for his understanding.

Being given a holiday when she least expected it revitalized her. More than anything in the world she wanted to see Peter and Michael again. And, if she dared to admit it, she wanted to see Dr. Wolfe. There was no getting around that fact. She felt like a teenager, mooning over a boy. *Only Jarod Wolfe was no boy.* He was a man like no other man she'd ever met in her life. But at twenty-seven, she shouldn't be reacting with such weak-kneed excitement at the mere thought of another meeting with him!

After talking to Carter, Domini phoned Marge at the office to see if anyone had left messages for her. She was aware of a fluttery sensation in her stomach as she wondered if there had been a call from the children's father—which was absurd, considering how they'd parted.

"You've had several callers, Miss Loring," the receptionist answered in her efficient way. "Lyle Hobson has phoned a half dozen times at least and left numbers where you can reach him. Your neighbor has called twice to tell you she's holding several packages for you. Also, someone from Tacoma, a Mr. Rowley, called. He's most anxious to hear from you and left two numbers. Renate Moffit dropped by the studio hoping you could go to lunch. Your voice teacher is out of town for two weeks. Oh, yes—Peter Wolfe called two days ago."

Domini gripped the receiver more tightly. "What did he say, Marge?" she demanded anxiously, dismissing everything else from her mind.

"Not much. He wanted to know how long you'd be away on tour and sounded quite dejected that he couldn't talk to you, but he didn't leave a message."

Domini sat up in bed, hugging her knees. "If he calls again today, tell him I'll get in touch with him soon."

"I'll do that, Miss Loring. If you don't mind my saying so, you don't sound like yourself. I hope you haven't caught the flu."

"It's just a bad cold, but Carter told me to take a week off. I'll call again as soon as I'm back in Seattle."

Restlessness seized Domini after they said goodbye. She knew Peter needed to talk, and the knowl-

edge tugged at her relentlessly. She could appreciate
the fact that he hadn't been able to put the episode out
of his mind. Until he apologized, it would weigh on his
conscience; he was his father's son, after all.

Perhaps she should call him now. But if Dr. Wolfe
answered, he might say something sarcastic and hang
up, making matters between them even worse. Then it
came to her: what she really needed to do was see Peter
in person! Why not surprise him and stop in
Bremerton before returning to Seattle? She could relax just as well at a hotel on the bay as she could anywhere else. And Dr. Wolfe wouldn't be able to fault
her for not keeping her promise to Michael and Peter
if she arrived on their doorstep!

Her mind made up, Domini called ahead to make a
reservation at the Coast Inn for the following day and
enjoyed the luxury of being driven there by Bill in the
company limousine. She slept most of the way, having plied herself with over-the-counter cold remedies
and cough medicine.

They arrived at the hotel late in the afternoon. Mist
shrouded the quaint port town, obscuring the view
from the hotel steps, but Domini's head was too congested for her to smell the salt spray in the air as Bill
helped her inside with her bags. He insisted on getting her settled before he departed for Seattle. Domini urged him to get home to his family before the fog
thickened, assuring him that she'd drive back to
Seattle in a rental car once she'd had a chance to visit
with Peter.

As soon as she was shown to her room, she put
through a call to Dr. Wolfe's home. To her keen disappointment she got his answering machine. The
message told her to call his office. Summoning her

courage once more, she dialed his office number and was told by his answering service to leave a message since it was Dr. Wolfe's day off. In case of emergency, callers were given a Dr. Hansen's number. Deflated that Jarod couldn't be reached, she left word that she'd checked into the hotel and would like to speak to Peter when it was convenient. Under no circumstances, did she want his father thinking she had the slightest desire to see *him*.

After a long soak in the bathtub, Domini slipped into a green-and-blue silk jersey dress and let herself out of the room. She craved something hot and wet to soothe her raw throat, but otherwise she had little appetite. If Peter phoned while she was in the dining room, the switchboard had been alerted to transfer the call there.

She caught sight of a dark-haired man bounding up the stairs two at a time as she started to descend them. He was dressed in an off-white cable-knit sweater and blue jeans, and moved with a natural, athletic grace she couldn't help but admire. Unexpectedly he paused to look up when he reached the first landing, and she gasped as their gazes collided. It was Dr. Wolfe!

The first thing that struck her was the intense blue of his eyes fastened unswervingly on her. He must have come directly from sailing. The wind had ruffled his brown hair and his cheeks showed signs of windburn. If she'd had any doubts about her feelings for this man, she could put them to rest now.

"You're really here," he finally murmured as if he couldn't believe it. His gaze passed with disturbing thoroughness over the high spots of color in her cheeks, the curves of her body, the dress swirling around her slender legs.

Domini hesitated, looking for censure in his eyes but finding none. If she hadn't known better, she could almost have imagined he was equally excited to see her. "I—I didn't mean to take you away from whatever you were doing. Your answering service said this was your day off." Haltingly, she started down the stairs toward him, afraid he would see the runaway pulse in her throat.

"The boat dock is in constant need of repair and I like any excuse that takes me away from it," he explained as she drew closer. "What are you doing here? I wasn't aware your tour extended to Bremerton."

Did she detect a trace of mockery in his tone? she wondered. Taking a deep breath, she moved down to the step just above his so they were at eye level. But it was a mistake. His nearness disturbed her far too much. "My tour was canceled. I decided this was a good time to visit Peter."

His searching gaze roamed over her face and a frown marred his features. "You're sick. How long have you been congested?"

"A few days."

A nerve began to hammer along his jaw. "I suppose I should thank the fates that made you ill for this unprecedented duty visit." He folded his arms across his broad chest in a totally masculine gesture. "The Story Princess succumbs to the common cold. You're mortal after all. Does Phillips know you're playing hooky?"

His taunt shouldn't have hurt so much when she'd come to expect his disdain, but she was determined to stay in control. "He told me to take the week off when he found out I was sick."

His mouth curved nastily. "I bet he doesn't know you're here in Bremerton."

His words infuriated her. "He has no say in my private life. I came because of Peter. If you've changed your mind about a meeting, then tell me now and I'll go back to Seattle this evening."

He stared at her through shuttered eyes. The remoteness of his manner extinguished any hope in her that he cared for her, even a little. "The boys were in the boat house with me when the message came on my beeper. They know you're in town," he told her, then glanced at his thick gold wristwatch. "I'll run by the house and get them. We'll come back and join you for dinner in the hotel dining room. You shouldn't be outside in this weather, and I suggest you go to bed right afterward. Are you on an antibiotic?"

His concern for her welfare confused her. "No, not yet."

"I'll bring you something when I come back. Why didn't Phillips make you see a doctor? I'm surprised such a shrewd businessman would allow his walking gold mine to go untended."

Afraid she'd say something that would shock the people coming up the stairs, she tried to step past him, but he blocked her way, waiting for the tourists to climb out of earshot.

"Domini..." He put a detaining hand on her arm. The sound of her name on his lips, more than the physical restraint, caused her to turn a pale face toward him. Lines darkened his features. "I shouldn't have mentioned Phillips. Strangely enough, I find myself wanting to protect the boys' gilded image of you. They're out of their minds with joy that you're here." His thumb traced circles on her heated skin.

"To be frank, I never expected you to call again, let alone come all the way here. The fact that you put yourself out for Peter's sake, when you should be home taking care of yourself, means more than you know." His hand seemed to slide away from her arm with reluctance. "I'll be back with the boys in a few minutes."

He dashed off, leaving a stunned Domini grasping the railing for support. In a matter of seconds, his unexpected gratitude had made her forget everything that had gone on before. He had no personal interest in her—that couldn't have been clearer—but his comments went a long way toward explaining his behavior.

His bias against celebrities must have come from his experience with his wife, Domini reasoned, though she certainly wasn't aware of the details. Perhaps his love for Amanda Carlson had filled him with resentment toward the career that took all her time—and her life. In any case, Domini felt sure that he never planned to see her again once Peter had made his peace with her. The knowledge filled her with a real sense of loss, a kind of physical and mental agony from which she didn't think she'd ever recover. Not when she'd fallen so deeply in love with him.

CHAPTER FIVE

DOMINI NEEDED to be alone, but she couldn't disappoint the children. And if she broke down now, they would see the ravages of her weeping. For their sake she felt she must keep her battle with their father private.

Returning to her room, she washed her face and put on fresh lipstick and blusher to hide the pallor of her complexion. Every meeting with Dr. Wolfe drained her a little more, but she had to conceal that from his children. After spraying on some Rochas perfume and giving her hair a quick brush, she went down to the dining area. An immense grate fire dominated one end of the room. Craving its warmth, she asked the hostess to seat their party near the fireplace. A strong wind had sprung up since her arrival; she could hear it moaning and beating against the windows and felt thankful to be inside.

It was still early for dinner and there were few tourists seated at the tables. While she waited for the boys and their father, she wandered around studying the many sketches and paintings hung on the walls. They portrayed the story of the boats and ships that had navigated the Sound. The place was a veritable museum of maritime lore.

"Where is she?" a familiar little voice called. Domini whirled around, more excited to see the children than she would have believed possible. But her spontaneous smile faded as she watched two pairs of bright blue eyes scan the few people in the room. It suddenly dawned on her that, like their father, they supposed she was a blonde because they'd never seen her except in full costume and wig.

Jarod's unnerving gaze found hers across the room. Her eyes must have signaled her distress because he bent and whispered something to the boys. They both looked her way at the same time, but still seemed hesitant.

Domini took in the sight of the three of them. They were dressed alike in sweaters and jeans. A lump lodged in her throat. She felt a sharply painful yearning to belong to that privileged little group.

"Should I go back for my wig?" She smiled tenderly as she walked toward them and held out her hands. Michael clutched his father's arm and stared, but Peter stepped forward and shook one hand, his eyes not quite meeting hers.

"Hello, Miss Loring." He bit his lip. "I-I'm sorry for what I did," he blurted out unexpectedly, a sheen of tears coating his eyes. Domini could see he was on the verge of breaking down completely.

Compassion for the boy made her throat close up. He'd obviously been miserable for a long time and she wished she'd made more of an effort to see him sooner. "Now let me think. What did you do?" she asked gently.

Peter lifted his dark blond head and eyed her fearfully.

"Do you know," Domini continued, "I can't remember. And once I can't remember something, I can never remember it again."

At first he simply looked at her in disbelief, then his cheeks dimpled, and suddenly he was laughing. The tears had gone.

"How about a hug, Peter? I've missed you." He needed no prodding this time and grasped her around her slender waist. His head lolled back and the smile he flashed filled her with happiness.

"Do you know what?" He stared at her hair. "Daddy's right. You don't look anything like my mom without your wig."

"No." She smiled back, trying to set the boys at ease. "But you do."

"Does he really?" Michael suddenly piped up and ran to her. Unhampered without her costume, she swept him into her arms.

"Yes. And so do you. Carbon copies, both of you."

"What's carbon copies?" He touched her black curls wonderingly.

For a fraction of a second she caught their father's glance. Unbelievably, his eyes were sending her a message of gratitude, and somehow the ugliness of those first few minutes on the stairs faded. He adored his children and must have loved his wife desperately. A searing pain shot through her body. *It couldn't be jealousy!* It just couldn't be! But she was very much afraid it was.

The children were still waiting for an answer to their question. "It means that the two of you resemble your mother so completely, no one in the world could ever mistake you for anyone else's children."

The boys smiled secretly at each other and then Michael unexpectedly kissed her. "Did you know her?"

She cleared her throat. "No. But I saw her on television. She was very lovely and very intelligent, just like you. And I think she was the most fortunate woman in the world to have two fine sons. In fact, you're one of the most fortunate families I know.''

"We are?" they both said in unison.

She didn't dare look at Jarod. In her mind he'd ceased to be Dr. Wolfe since they'd encountered each other on the hotel stairs. "I know you've lost your mother and nothing will ever replace her. But your father is still alive and he loves you very much.'' She swallowed hard. "My mother died when I was a teenager and my daddy took care of me and loved me, just like your daddy. But he died more than a year ago.''

"Now you're all alone,'' Michael said wistfully, his pale gold head resting against her shoulder.

"No, she's not,'' Peter argued manfully. "You've got us, haven't you, Miss Loring? Hasn't she, Daddy?'' He glanced at his father for confirmation.

"It certainly looks that way,'' came the dry retort over his children's heads, but Domini detected the hidden mockery. "Peter, you have to remember that Miss Loring is a grown-up and she's got all kinds of friends clamoring to take care of her. We'd make up the end of a very long line, I'm afraid.''

The room swam as Domini digested another insult. Or was it a warning to keep her distance with his children? "Are you boys hungry? I know I am.'' She set Michael on the floor, and still holding his hand ushered him to the table.

"Liar,'' Jarod whispered at her back. He pulled out her chair and arranged the boys at either side. Then he took his place across the table from her.

She picked up the menu, hardly seeing it, but anxious to look anywhere except at him. "What do you boys recommend?''

"We *boys* recommend the hot chowder for you," Jarod said and drew a bottle of pills from his pocket. "Take two of these now, and one every four hours until they're gone." He placed them by her water goblet.

"You sound pretty sick, Miss Loring. Daddy says you have to go to bed after dinner," Peter offered.

"Are you going to do what he says?"

Domini turned to Michael. "Well, I don't know for sure. He's not my daddy," she teased, squeezing his hand.

"I know. But I think he'd like to be. He said he'd put you to bed himself if you don't do what you're told. He can be awfully scary."

"I'll just bet." Domini shot Jarod a speaking glance.

His blue eyes fused with hers. "It seems I'm to be forever quoted by my children. Fortunately for you, that problem will no longer exist after you leave Bremerton."

His mild tone didn't deceive her. He was telling her that now she'd allowed Peter to get things off his chest, she could leave anytime. The sooner the better.

At this juncture the waitress came to the table and started taking orders. As soon as she'd left, the conversation focused on the boys' plans to spend the next day with Domini.

"We want to take you to Bainbridge Island, Miss Loring," Peter started in immediately. "Andy goes over there all the time with his grandma and says it's really fun on the ferry. Is that all right with you, Dad?"

Jarod nodded. "Provided she's well enough, which I seriously doubt." But his comment didn't dampen their spirits as they made their plans.

Dinner arrived and Domini tried the soup, but after a few mouthfuls, she simply couldn't manage any more. Her appetite had deserted her, and it didn't help that Jarod rarely took his eyes from her face. She toyed with her spoon and drank hot coffee while the others tucked into their halibut.

"Time for bed, I think," Jarod said a while later as the boys started on their sherbet. "Say good-night to Miss Loring." He got up from his seat and came around to help her from the table. He must have known she longed for bed.

"Already?" Peter frowned. "It's only seven-thirty."

Jarod's hands caressed her waist, unintentionally she was sure, but she trembled. "Miss Loring should have been in bed hours ago."

"If I get my rest tonight, I'll be able to go with you on that ferry ride to Bainbridge Island in the morning," she said lightly attempting to placate the children.

"Only if you're feeling a hundred percent better," Jarod interjected. "Right now I'd say you're too sick to make any plans."

"Daddy?" Michael asked. "When Miss Loring gets well, *please* will you take us all sailing? You'd love it!" he told her earnestly, hugging her leg and smiling up at her.

"I'm afraid that's out of the question, Mike," Jarod answered before Domini could say a word. "Now, you two wait here for me. I won't be long."

"Please be better tomorrow," Michael pleaded with real concern showing in his cornflower-blue eyes. "I want to stay with you tonight. Can I?'' He turned to his father for permission.

"I'm afraid not tonight," Domini said, not giving Jarod the chance to speak for her again. She bent down to hug Michael. "But I'll see you tomorrow."

"Can we call you in the morning?" Peter wanted to know, the rest of his dessert forgotten.

"Yes, of course." She patted his soft cheek and dropped a kiss on Michael's head. "I should be feeling much better by morning with your father taking such good care of me."

"Don't count on it," Jarod whispered, urging her forward. The warmth of his hand against her back gave her a yielding sense of delight.

"Good night, children," she murmured, still brooding on their crestfallen faces as Jarod accompanied her to her room.

To her surprise he'd brought a small humidifier, which had been placed on the table next to the bed. All of this must have been accomplished while she studied the pictures in the dining room. Despite the disapproval that he exhibited, she felt safe and cared for. She wanted to curl up in his arms, beg him to be kind to her and then fall asleep, knowing that when she woke he'd still be there holding her.

"You're dead on your feet. I want you in bed right away." The authoritative ring of his voice reminded her that he was speaking as a doctor, and it brought her up short.

"As soon as you leave."

He rubbed the back of his neck, a mannerism he didn't seem to be aware of. "Call me if you have any difficulty during the night. I want your promise on that."

Domini nodded without looking at him. "Thank you for your help."

"It's my job."

"Thank you anyway." The man was impossible.

"Domini—"

She lifted her head at the odd inflection in his voice and saw surprising look of concern on his face.

He moved toward her and put a cool hand to her forehead. "You're running a temperature. I don't like it."

She swayed a little at his touch. "I'll be fine in the morning. It was foolish of me not to see a doctor when I first realized my cold wasn't going away."

He shook his head. "You shouldn't have attempted to visit Peter. You should have waited until you felt better."

They stood so close she could see the faint growth of beard on his chin. "I didn't want to put him off any longer. When Marge told me he called the studio, I knew he was suffering."

Jarod stiffened. "Peter phoned you?"

"Yes, and I can imagine how he felt. Once you make up your mind to apologize for something, you need to do it right away, while you still have the courage."

"That's very perceptive of you. Where did you learn so much about children?"

"What do you mean?"

"For the past week I've worried myself sick that Peter might never forgive himself for the trouble he caused. In some ways, he's almost too conscientious. But one succinct comment and a smile from you, and his face is like sunshine, the nightmare forgotten. You have a gift for relating to children, I'll give you that."

And nothing else, she mused sadly. "I'm glad he's out of his misery."

His brow furrowed. "It's time to put you out of yours. I'll say good-night." He walked to the table and turned on the humidifier, then glanced at her over his shoulder. "I hope you realize that if you're still running a temperature tomorrow, you won't be going anywhere. The boys have a dozen plans in mind, but I'll warn them tonight that you may be in no condition to do anything other than lie in bed for the next few days."

Domini closed her eyes, fighting the impulse to beg him to stay with her for a while. In a frighteningly short time, he'd become necessary to her existence. "Why don't we wait and see what the day brings?"

"I already have a fair idea," he said gravely. Still, he seemed reluctant to go. "I'll leave word at the desk how to get in touch with me in case there's an emergency."

"Are you trying to frighten me?" She accompanied the words by a wan smile as he made his way to the door. With one hand on the door handle, he turned to face her.

"Maybe. I've seen conditions like yours change into pneumonia overnight. You've been driving yourself way too hard for a long time. Your type always does. Good night, Miss Loring."

Domini wanted to scream at the man's presumption, but it would have come out a squeak. She did the next best thing and kicked off one shoe so it banged against the door he'd just closed. The childish action only served to show her how quickly things had degenerated to out-and-out war once again.

She slipped out of her clothes and pulled on a brief cotton nightgown, not wanting to wear anything heavier, feeling this feverish. The eiderdown comforter stifled her and she pushed it to the foot of the bed, making do with the sheet. She'd been so sleepy over dinner she'd feared her head would fall in the chowder.

Now that she was in bed, every word, every nuance of her exchange with Jarod passed through her mind, making sleep impossible. She felt so wretched she wanted to howl but her cold had grown so much worse she could hardly even breathe.

She turned on her side so she could feel the vapor from the humidifier on her face and gradually it brought relief. Hot tears trickled out of the corners of her eyes. Jarod might not approve of her or like her, but he'd done everything in his power to make her comfortable and keep her sickness in check. His bedside manner couldn't be faulted. The tears slowly turned into sobs at the hopelessness of her situation. He wanted Domini out of Bremerton—out of his life—as soon as he could get her on her feet. She should never have come. A phone call to Peter would have sufficed. Jarod Wolfe was well and truly entrenched in her heart; there would be nothing but pain in any further contact.

When the phone rang, Domini awoke with a shock. She thought it was still early, until she glanced at her watch, which said nine in the morning. The humidifier had shut off at some point during the night. She reached for the receiver, expecting to hear one of the boys' voices, and said hello. Her voice was two registers lower than normal.

"You sound exactly as I expected," Jarod answered. "Were you able to sleep?"

"Yes. The steam helped a lot. Thank you."

"You need to take another pill right now and then one every four hours. I don't want you going anywhere today. Are you still feverish?"

Domini didn't need to feel her cheeks to know she still had a temperature. "I think it's down," she lied. "I'm really feeling much better after the good night's sleep. You don't need to worry about me."

"I'm glad to hear your temp's no worse but you must take care! If you've improved even more by tomorrow, then we'll see about your getting up. Drink plenty of liquids today and keep the humidifier going. I'm at the hospital right now, and I'll probably be here the rest of the morning. If you should need me, call the switchboard and they'll page me."

"I-I'm sure I won't need anything, but thank you for all your help and concern."

There was a slight pause. "All the thanks I want is to see you feeling better so you can go over to the island with the boys and then back to your work in Seattle. Don't forget to take your medicine." He said goodbye and rang off.

Domini sat up in the bed, still clutching the receiver. He couldn't wait to see the last of her!

Well, he was going to get his wish. By evening she'd be on her way back to Seattle. But first she planned to spend some time with the children.

After taking another pill and showering, she got dressed, packed and arranged with the front desk for a rental car to be put at her disposal later in the day. Then she made inquiries about departure times for the ferry to Bainbridge Island. She and the boys could hop

over there for a few hours, have a big lunch and return in time for dinner. That would keep her out of
Jarod's reach all day and give her time to enjoy the
boys, since she'd probably never see them again.

On the ferry ride she could lie back in one of the
lounge chairs and relax while the children found ways
to entertain themselves. No matter how ill she felt, she
couldn't possibly stay alone in a hotel room with
nothing to do but think about him, and she couldn't
leave Bremerton without seeing the children. This was
the only solution that made sense.

Domini waited at the terminal for Mrs. Maughan to
bring the boys. Typical weather prevailed—patches of
fog and penetrating cold. Not the best conditions for
an outing, but Domini didn't mind. She'd checked out
of the hotel, paid her bill and left her bags and the
humidifier with the clerk at the front desk. She'd also
left an envelope addressed to Dr. Wolfe, containing a
thank-you note and a check to cover the cost of her
dinner and the prescription. She didn't think she'd left
anything undone.

She felt a positively maternal twinge as she watched
the boys scramble out of the family car and run toward her. She waved to Mrs. Maughan before hugging Peter and Michael and ushering them into the
building.

"This won't be quite as exciting as sailing on your
father's boat, but I know we'll have a wonderful time
just the same."

Michael jumped up and down with excitement as
they lined up to board the vessel, which would take
them to Seattle, where they'd transfer to the ferry for
Bainbridge Island. "Daddy's never taken us to the
island on this ferry before because he says there's no

point when we have a *perfectly* good one of our own."
His imitation of Jarod was so priceless Domini burst
out laughing, which aggravated her cough.

"My friend, Andy, says they have slot machines on
board. Can we play them, Miss Loring?"

Domini wasn't sure how Jarod would feel about
that, but right now she was prepared to indulge his
children and couldn't see that it would harm them.
"Why not?"

"Goody!" the boys cheered.

"We brought our own spending money," Peter offered. Together they showed her the change in their
pockets with a look of such excitement she couldn't
have said no. "But please don't tell Dad," Peter
begged.

"I'll have to tell him the truth if he asks," Domini
explained. "But maybe he won't."

The boys grinned. "I'm glad you're feeling better
today," Peter said as they watched the ferry move
away from the dock. "Daddy said you'd have to stay
in bed today."

"That's because he thought I'd be worse, but as you
can see, I'm fine. When we get to the island, we'll hunt
for a fun place to have lunch. What do you say?" The
smiles on their faces left nothing to the imagination.
"One more thing. Keep your life preservers on the
whole time. Okay?"

They nodded, then skipped off to explore the ferry.
An hour later, after boarding the second ferry, they
ran to find the slot machines.

Despite the rough water and encroaching fog, the
ferry made excellent time. Peter and Michael chatted
nonstop as the three of them wandered in and out of
the island's stores. They had a leisurely lunch; al-

though Domini could barely manage tea and toast, the boys stuffed themselves with donuts and hot chocolate after hamburgers. She bought them each a book and then it was time to take the ferry back to Seattle.

The weather had grown worse as they explored the island. A strong wind blew steadily, bringing with it more cold and rain. Domini felt miserable to the point of exhaustion. The choppy water didn't help her increasing nausea. Though the common rooms were warm and she drank several cups of coffee to ease her throat, a tightness had settled in her chest and she coughed continually.

Michael and Peter were so excited by the day's activities, they didn't notice how weak she'd become as they boarded the ferry for the return trip to Bremerton. It was a fight to make them wear their life preservers, since none of the other children were wearing them. But when she explained that she loved them and wanted to know they were all right when they were out of her sight, they yielded to her entreaty. Then, sounding just like his father, Peter insisted she wear one, too. A smile lifted the corner of her drawn mouth despite her misery as she conceded his point and donned an adult life preserver.

Domini watched the children for almost an hour, then wandered out on deck for some fresh air. The ferry seemed to be marooned in a sea of fog. She doubted they were making very good time back to port. The whitecaps were much worse on the return trip and she had to brace herself against the pitch and roll of the vessel.

She thought they must be near port because she suddenly heard the sound of the buoys. She longed to get back to the hotel room and lie down; she realized now that she should have taken Jarod's advice. Then she remembered she'd given up her hotel room. While she was berating herself for her foolishness and trying to decide whether she should attempt the drive home, the foghorn blasted, making her jump. It was quickly followed by another long series of blasts and then the ship's siren.

Some unnamed dread sent a thrill of fear through her body. She turned instinctively toward the lounge where she'd left the children playing. In that instant she saw the bow of another vessel ram the back of the ferry.

Like some eerie ghost ship in a nightmare it had appeared out of nowhere, looming sinister and dark. At the moment of impact the ferry staggered, rose up and then plunged downward. Domini didn't have the strength to hang on to the railing and felt herself being thrown headlong into the churning waters along with several other passengers who'd been standing by her on the deck.

Her horrified scream came out a gurgle as a wall of seawater closed over her head. She was briefly conscious of a sharp pain in her arm. The last thing she remembered, before everything went black, was the children.

DOMINI AWOKE to the sound of sirens. She forced open her eyes and discovered herself lying in an ambulance with an oxygen mask over her face. When she lifted her hand to push it away, she saw that the needle of an IV had been inserted in her right arm. She noticed the gauze taped to her other arm, and it was then that she became aware of the pain.

Suddenly she remembered the accident with terrifying clarity. She clutched the arm of the attendant who was adjusting the blood pressure cuff. "Michael, Peter!" she screamed. "Please, help me. I've got to find them." She struggled to sit up, but the attendant gently urged her back against the stretcher.

"Try to calm down. Everything possible is being done to locate all the passengers and get them safely to hospital. Are they your children?"

"No," she groaned as tears streamed down her cheeks. "M-Michael's only five. Please, I've got know if they've been found. Help me," she called out hysterically.

"We'll inquire as soon as we get to the hospital. Now, try to—"

"You don't understand! Dr. Wolfe's already lost his wife. If anything happens to his children—" She brought a fist to her mouth, mindless of her injured arm. "It's all my fault." She broke down and sobbed uncontrollably.

The attendant placed his hands on her heaving shoulders. "You mean Dr. Jarod Wolfe's boys were on board?"

"Yes!" she cried, thrashing about in an effort to sit up. "He'll be frantic. I've got to know they're alive!"

Domini could hear the man speaking to the driver, who relayed the information over the ambulance radio.

"We've notified the hospital and the harbor police. The victims have been taken to various clinics and emergency centers in the surrounding areas. I believe the children were picked up first. No fatalities have been reported, if that will ease your mind."

"I made them wear life preservers," she said, her voice shaking.

"Then you've got nothing to worry about. From what I understand, most of the passengers were inside the ferry when the collision occurred and they weren't affected like those out on deck."

She nodded. "That's where I was when it happened. I should never have taken them out today." She began weeping all over again. "Please call in and find out if there's been any word."

"The hospital entrance is straight ahead. We'll have answers for you within a few minutes."

With an efficiency she could scarcely credit, Domini was wheeled into the emergency wing, where a flock of nurses and doctors had converged to aid the victims. Someone rolled her into a cubicle and moved her onto an examining table.

She begged the attending physician to make inquiries about the children. He assured her that everything humanly possible was being done to locate them, as well as Dr. Wolfe. But she wouldn't be consoled. The minutes stretched into hours.

Domini lay there in mental agony, hardly aware that a doctor was putting stitches in her arm. If anything had happened to either of the boys, life wouldn't be worth living. She closed her eyes and prayed harder than she'd ever prayed in her life, doubling up as a paroxysm of coughing shook her.

"I'm going to do a few cultures," a technician explained, shutting the curtains on her way out.

The lab work seemed to take forever. Domini stared at the ceiling until tears blurred her vision once more. A sense of hopelessness drove her into deeper despair. She'd rather die than see the look on Jarod's face if anything had happened to his children.

When she heard the sound of the curtains being pushed aside, she struggled to raise herself onto her good arm. "Please, someone's got to help me. Have the Wolfe children been found?"

A tall figure wearing a white lab coat and stethoscope moved to the side of the bed. She assumed it was one of the doctors she had already seen until she looked up into the familiar blue eyes, now shadowed with intense pain. "Jarod!"

CHAPTER SIX

HER FRIGHTENED EYES searched his and what she read there caused something to shrivel inside her. "The children—"

"They're fine, Domini." His statement should have reassured her, but there was so much emotion behind his words, she felt he had to be keeping something from her.

"Don't spare me, Jarod. Tell me the truth!" She was horrified by his unnatural pallor, by the deep lines of pain and worry carved into his face. "It's my fault. Everything," she agonized, moving her head from side to side, unable to bear the pain. "Why didn't I die?"

His hands caught her face and stilled the frantic movement. He forced her to look up at him. "Did you hear what I said? Nothing happened to the boys. They're home safe and sound, eating dinner with Mrs. Maughan at this very moment."

"I-I can't believe it. They're really home?" Hot fresh tears spilled down her cheeks and over his hands as she spoke.

"Shall I bring in the harbormaster? He found them perched on top of the piano in the lounge, waiting for the lifeboats. Their feet never even got wet."

She made a funny little noise in her throat. "The piano?" In her mind's eye she could see the ancient baby grand in a corner of the lounge.

The rigid mouth of a moment ago relaxed into a grin. She'd never seen Jarod smile like that before. "I've taught the boys well. Always go for the high ground."

He couldn't possibly joke like this if he weren't telling the truth. It shone from his brilliant blue eyes and dissolved her burden of guilt and anguish. "Thank God, Jarod." A little sob escaped. "Th-they're safe."

"They are." Then his dark head lowered and the mouth she'd hungered for closed over hers in a kiss of unexpected gentleness. It didn't last long enough. "Now the trick is to convince my children that you're alive and in one piece, and I can't very well do that until we get you taken care of."

The tenderness of his touch was almost her undoing as he smoothed the limp black tendrils from her forehead. "I'm putting you in a private room as soon as we get a chest X ray. We'll give you something for your cough in a few minutes."

Her hand clutched his. "I don't think I could bear to stay in the hospital. Couldn't I go back to the hotel if I promise to follow your instructions to the letter?"

His face wore its grim expression again. "You need complete rest, something you probably haven't had for years. There's a possibility you've come down with pneumonia, but don't be frightened." He followed the line of her cheeks, her jaw with the back of his finger. "I won't let anything happen to you." His promise reassured her; she was grateful for his concern about her physical condition. But his words, his touch, had started a fierce, new ache, one that X rays couldn't discern and penicillin couldn't cure.

"I'm not afraid, but it seems like yesterday that I was at the hospital sitting by my father's bedside after his heart attack. This place is a morbid reminder," she explained and ended on a coughing spell.

His brows drew together. "When, exactly, did he die?"

She swallowed with difficulty. "A year ago last August."

"I didn't realize, somehow, that it had been so recent," he said, almost to himself. "Did you give yourself time to recover afterward, to grieve and come to terms with his death?"

Domini shrugged.

"That's just what I should have expected." His voice was harsh. "No doubt you drove yourself harder than ever when—"

"I had responsibilities, a job to do," she retorted. "I—" Heavens! Her job! No one at the studio had any idea of her whereabouts now that she'd checked out of the hotel.

"I'm going to see if they've got your results," he said abruptly, and turned to leave.

She called him back. "Jarod?"

He looked anxiously in her direction and moved to her side immediately. "What is it? What's wrong?"

She moistened her dry lips. "Would it be too much trouble to phone Carter?"

Her request froze him into immobility. For a moment he said nothing, but his mouth went white around the edges. "Do you need him, Domini?"

A strange tension pervaded the atmosphere, as if her answer mattered in some way she didn't understand. "No," she finally said, "but he should be told what's happened. He's in the process of making plans for me to go to Spokane to do another Story Princess tour as soon as I get back."

His mouth tightened. "If you have pneumonia, it could be several months before I allow you to return to work, let alone undertake another tour that could put you in even worse shape than you are right now!"

She lifted her head. "Please don't tell Carter that— not in those exact words, anyway. If he could simply be notified that I might need another week before I can go home..."

Jarod's blue eyes glittered dangerously as his body tautened. "Carter Phillips needs to be told the facts. It's time he realized you've been overextending yourself and *this* is the result!" He stood there like an avenging prince and she shivered beneath the cotton drape. "You pack more into a day than most people manage in a whole week! Television shows and personal appearances—recording—contests... When is there time for Domini Loring *the woman*?"

Domini blinked. Did he really envision her life like that? "I came here with no other thought than to visit the children and enjoy myself."

"For a day and a night, you mean?" came the sarcastic rejoinder. "And when you fulfilled your obligation to the boys, you'd hurry back to Phillips and all his plans for you."

She closed her eyes in frustration. "That wasn't my intention, Jarod."

He raked a hand through his dark hair. "You don't convince me. I happen to know you couldn't wait to be gone from here. You disobeyed my advice and actually checked out of your hotel. You lied through your teeth when you told me your temperature was down."

"Because I didn't want to disappoint the children by staying in bed all day. I just couldn't do that to them, and since you'd started me on the antibiotic, I thought it wouldn't do any harm.''

All of which was true enough, but she couldn't possibly tell him her *real* reason—or he'd know she was hopelessly in love with him. She couldn't confess that she wanted him so desperately, it was pure torture to be this close to him.

"How do you explain the rental car?" His quiet anger was somehow more frightening than his earlier outburst.

Domini stared at him in astonishment. How did he know about that? Nothing seemed to escape his notice.

"Dr. Wolfe? We're ready in X ray." A young, towheaded orderly pulled the curtain aside to address Jarod. For Domini, the intrusion couldn't have come at a more welcome moment.

Jarod's dark head jerked around and he gave the young man a brief nod. "Tell Matthew I want the result of her X rays the minute they're ready."

"Yes, sir!"

BETWEEN PAINKILLERS for her arm and medication for her cough, Domini slept on and off for the next forty-eight hours, scarcely cognizant of what went on around her. Jarod came to her private room at odd intervals of the day and night to check on her, but kept their conversation to a minimum, insisting she have total rest.

It occurred to Domini that Jarod might be right about her driving herself too hard. People often commented that she possessed her father's trait of taking her obligations seriously, never letting people down. When she thought about it, she couldn't recall a time when either of her parents had truly relaxed. It wasn't in their natures. They seemed to feel guilty if they weren't working at something.

Domini didn't think her attitude was quite that extreme, but it *had* been several years since she'd done anything that even resembled taking a vacation. Somehow the idea of traveling alone held little appeal. But when she recovered from this, she'd arrange a holiday and go lie on a beach somewhere, just soaking up sun.

Helen Andelin, her friend and colleague for the past three years at Children's Playhouse, went to Maui every winter with her husband. She'd repeatedly urged Domini to travel with them. Domini, not wanting to intrude, had always declined.

But the more she thought about it, the more attractive an island vacation sounded. She'd be able to swim and sunbathe and read to her heart's content. No deadlines, no pressures. And maybe, by some miracle, she'd learn to live without Jarod Wolfe.

The following morning she awakened to a room full of flowers. Her eyes misted over as she read the cards and expressions of love from everyone at the studio. It meant Jarod had made the phone call to Carter.

Allen's card had her smiling. "Dear Beauty—" his pet name for her "—if that *wolf* so much as hurts one hair on your lovely head, he'll have to answer to me." She sighed. If only Allen knew how expertly Jarod watched over her.

Carter had sent white carnations, his standard. The card read, "Take all the time you need. When you're ready, I'll come for you. Carter."

Jarod's noon visit coincided with a long-distance phone call from Lyle Hobson, who'd called the studio and found out about the accident. Jarod's impatience to talk to her forced Domini to cut the phone call short, which was probably a good thing because Lyle was anxious to discuss the singing engagements the oratorio society had lined up for the winter season. Now that she was ill, she couldn't commit herself to anything.

She liked Lyle and knew that he more than liked her. But she never went out with him or encouraged anything other than a mild friendship. There had always been something lacking—the same missing element that had prevented her from marrying long before now. Only she'd never been able to figure out what that elusive quality was—until Jarod Wolfe swept into her life, playing havoc with her emotions.

She hung up the phone and then turned to Jarod, who was smiling mysteriously. All at once, he produced an exquisite little tree brimming with blood-red rose buds. A few had burst into bloom. She'd never seen anything so beautiful except in fairy-tale illustrations. Hands trembling, she reached for the card, it read, "For a real live princess. Love, Peter and Michael."

She leaned forward and buried her nose in the flowers, forgetting she couldn't smell their fragrance. The miniature roses were a marvel. No doubt the boys had wanted to do something for her, but it had been Jarod who'd seen to it, Jarod who'd conceived of such an unusual and beautiful gift.

"I have a present, as well, in case you were wondering." His deep rich voice broke in on her thoughts. She fell back against the pillow, overwhelmed and touched by his continued generosity and thoughtfulness.

"You've done far too much for me already." Their eyes finally met. He looked incredibly male and appealing in a coffee-brown turtleneck and darker brown trousers. No sign of the doctor today. "The rose tree is beautiful and I adore it."

As she spoke, he was busy making a place for it among the other flowers on the utility table. "You have many admirers, apart from Peter and Michael."

"But none as important as your children," she blurted out, not wanting to hear another nasty remark from him at a time like this. "When the phone rang a few minutes ago, I was disappointed not to hear one of them on the other end. You've told them not to call me, haven't you?"

He approached the bed and stood there, studying her chart. "I thought it best to wait until I had the results of all your tests."

"And?" Her heartbeat quickened.

"That's *my* present." He lifted his head and for the second time, looked directly into her eyes. "Everything came back negative, which means you don't have pneumonia."

"Thank heaven!" A full, unguarded smile broke out on her face. "I owe it all to you."

The smile he gave her in return suddenly transformed his whole face. "There's more to my present. In a few minutes, the nurse will be in to help you dress, because I'm taking you home with me."

"What did you say?"

"You have bronchitis and need to be watched closely for the next couple of weeks. Barring any complications, you should start to improve rapidly after that *if* you obey my orders and do nothing but rest.

"I know how much you've disliked being in the hospital, so I thought you'd do better at the house. If you're under my roof, I'll know my instructions are being carried out. You need someone to look after you, and who better than Mrs. Maughan? She's retired now, but she was a nurse before she came to work for me. Between the two of us, you ought to recover."

Domini looked away, unable to take it all in. Her wildest dream was about to come true. But the instant she realized this, she was already mourning the day she'd have to leave and go back to Seattle. She knew instinctively that it would be like tearing her heart from her body. She couldn't risk that kind of pain, no matter how much, how badly, she wanted to accept his offer.

"Is the idea so distasteful to you?"

The abruptness of his question brought her head around. "I think I'm in shock," she whispered, afraid to hope, even for a moment, that she'd detected hurt in his voice. "It would disrupt your whole life to have me there."

He rubbed his chin. "What if I told you Peter sees this as a way to make up for everything that's happened?"

Domini didn't understand. "He's already apologized."

"He feels responsible because he's the one who brought up the outing to Bainbridge in the first place—all because of the slot machines."

Her eyes widened. Poor Peter. "I don't understand. What does that have to do with anything? I played the machines myself!" she said, hastening to defend the children.

"If you think he felt guilty about the lie he wrote for the contest, you should see the state he's in *now*. He feels responsible for your condition."

"But that's absurd. If anything, I'm the one who should be begging forgiveness for putting your children in such terrible danger in the first place."

His mouth hardened. "They sail with me most weekends and have been in worse situations. You couldn't have predicted the freak accident that caused the collision. No one could have. If I seemed upset, it was because you were in that freezing water with a temperature. Thank God you were wearing a life preserver. It saved your life, Domini!"

"Thanks to Peter."

"What?" His eyes blazed with blue light.

"He insisted I wear one when I told the boys they had to keep preservers on the whole time. He reminds me of you." She flashed him a smile, hoping to soften his mood, but he appeared caught up in his own tortured thoughts.

"Four people are still unaccounted for since the accident. When I think—" His hands tightened into fists at his sides.

Domini bowed her head. "All I've done is think about your adorable children and what might have happened." She covered her face with her hands as she imagined them drowning not two miles from shore, within sight of their home on the hillside. "I suppose this has come too soon after the other incident for Peter to handle," she murmured, glancing up at Jarod.

"I think everyone might heal if you come to our home to recuperate. All debts will be paid in full."

Their eyes caught and held. "If you're sure this will help Peter and won't cause you too much trouble, I can't imagine anything more wonderful than being surrounded by my two favorite children and Bremerton's most celebrated doctor." Her smile widened mischievously. "The nurses gossip nonstop about you, Jarod. You must know that."

He rolled his eyes. "Obviously, the sooner I get you out of here the better. I promised you'd be home when the children returned from school this afternoon."

She swallowed the lump in her throat. "Jarod, you're rearranging your whole life for me and I feel so helpless."

His blue eyes studied her intently, but his voice was clinical, detached. "Sometimes that's not such a bad thing. Giving up the need to be constantly in control may even have a positive effect on your health, not to mention your state of mind. I prescribe plenty of rest, freedom from responsibility, good food and fresh sea air."

"If you continue to treat me like royalty, you might not be able to get rid of me when the time comes. Have you thought of that?" She had to make a joke of it or go a little mad.

"You'd receive no dissenting vote from the children's corner. I can assure you of that."

Domini pretended great interest in the IV attachment. "Won't my presence in your home create unwanted gossip?"

"I hope so." He threw her a heart-stopping smile. "In fact, I'm rather hoping the rumors about a beautiful woman living in my home spread far and wide—or at least as far as my clinic."

She failed to see the humor in it. "It could hurt your reputation. I wouldn't want that on my conscience."

"On the contrary. Curiosity will be good for business."

"That's not funny, Jarod. From what I've heard you have to turn people away as it is. You don't need that kind of following."

"It's good for my image," he persisted lightly. "People will have to rethink the possibilities. Has the local doctor finally stopped grieving and found a new interest? Every scandalized busybody for miles around will have a field day. The beautiful part is that no one knows who you really are. I'll be harboring a mystery woman—no one will guess there's a real princess hidden in the wolf's lair...."

His teasing disturbed her and she decided not to respond to it. "My traveler's cheques are with my luggage." She spoke as matter-of-factly as possible, fighting to keep the tremor out of her voice. "If I could have them, I can pay my bill."

He moved over to the door. "It's been taken care of. While the nurse prepares you for travel, I'll find someone to help load all these flowers."

"I'd rather leave them. Maybe the nurses can give them to some of the other patients. The only gift I want is the rose tree."

He went very still. "You're sure?"

"I'd like to have it forever. If I can keep it alive until summer, I'd like to take it to Tacoma and plant it in the front flower bed."

One eyebrow arched. "Your family home?"

"Yes. After Father died, I was urged to sell the house, but Carter advised me to hold on to it. At the last minute I took his advice. There are too many good memories associated with home. I try to go there as often as I can."

He seemed pensive. "So you were on your way back from Tacoma while I haunted your office that Monday?"

"Yes."

"I'll be back for you in a while." He shifted his weight. "I hope you don't mind that I went through your bags to find something for you to wear today. Unfortunately, the clothes you had on at the time of the accident were too badly damaged to wear again."

She murmured her thanks, hardly able to breathe as she imagined him handling her personal things. It seemed so . . . intimate an act.

"You travel lightly for a woman."

She took a deep breath. "I'm the Story Princess. All I really need is my costume."

Rich laughter rumbled out of him. "I never thought I'd live to see the day I'd hear a woman say that. You're so full of surprises I can't keep up with you. However, I should tell you that I didn't see the costume among your clothes."

"That's because Bill took it back to Seattle with him."

"Another admirer?" His eyes glinted.

"The security man at the studio. He's a grandfather several times over," she said, feeling a little defensive.

"They're the worst kind," he muttered sarcastically. With that, he strode out the door. She didn't have any more time to contemplate the wisdom of going home with him because the nurse swept into the room carrying Domini's nightgown and quilted robe.

Domini wondered if she still had any secrets from Jarod. If he ever bothered to really look, he'd recognize how much she loved him—and that frightened her. He might be appalled by the depth of her feeling. Or else he'd pity her. She couldn't tolerate either possibility.

"We'll be home within five minutes," Jarod confirmed as they drove away from the hospital half an hour later. Swirling mists made for poor visibility but Domini didn't care whether or not she saw her surroundings. Just being with him meant everything, and to think of "home" in connection with Jarod intensified the ache growing inside her.

They traveled in silence the rest of the way, passing through the heart of the town and proceeding north along the coastal highway. Jarod geared down and turned onto a private road leading to the house. She couldn't see any other homes and mentioned as much to Jarod, who told her he valued his privacy and had bought up several acres of land to ensure it.

Domini eyed the multistoried dwelling with great interest. It came as a total surprise at the end of a winding drive lined with rhododendrons and lush vegetation—a dove-gray structure blending traditional warmth and modern simplicity. Built to withstand gale-force winds and challenge the elements, it was certainly a fitting residence for someone like Jarod.

He parked the car and turned to Domini. "Mrs. Maughan must just have left to pick up the children. Let's get you inside and settled before they descend." With that male grace so characteristic of him, he helped Domini from the car, then picked her up in his arms, rose tree and all. His body provided warmth against the biting cold.

"I can walk," she whispered, acutely aware of his mouth hovering inches from her own. If she lifted her head a fraction...

"That's debatable." As he spoke the strong breeze off the Sound seemed to cut right through her. In the distance she heard the mournful sound of a foghorn and shuddered in remembrance.

Jarod's arms tightened around her. "Don't think about it anymore. You're safe now." He read her mind with practiced ease and held her closer to his heart.

Ice crunched underfoot as he walked the short distance to the entry of the house. "It's an exciting design," Domini said, her gaze following the chalk-white trim around the door and windows as he opened the door.

"I had it built after Amanda died. A kind of therapy, I suppose." The unexpected revelation distressed her, but she found some relief in knowing that the house wouldn't be haunted by the presence of a woman he'd idolized.

In a few strides he carried her down a hallway that opened into a sunken living room dominated by a stone fireplace. Reflections of firelight flickered on the oyster-colored walls and the deeper-toned blues and grays of two love seats and a couch placed near the hearth.

Domini was struck by the clean lines and the mood of serenity they achieved. Then she gasped. Still carrying her, Jarod had drawn near to the picture window that overlooked the huge bay. The room felt like an extension of the sea and sky, perched high on the hill like an eagle's aerie.

Her cry of wonder brought a smile to his lips. "Michael says his tummy falls to his feet when he looks out this window."

She tightened her hold around his neck. "Michael's right. It's the most spectacular view I've ever seen."

His warm breath fanned her black curls. "You haven't been upstairs yet."

The husky tone of his voice excited her unbearably. She'd be in serious trouble, she thought, if he decided to take her vital signs right then.

A spiral staircase rose to a large loft at the opposite end of the room, but Domini had only a fleeting glimpse of it before Jarod carried her up another flight of stairs to what could only be considered the master bedroom.

Her eyes immediately took in the wall of glass that revealed a sweeping panorama of sea and sky. A king-size bed rested against another wall opposite a fireplace. She could feel the warmth of the fire crackling merrily behind a polished brass firescreen. Above the bed were shelves built to the ceiling, stacked with books and tapes and medical journals. Jarod had a literal hideaway where he could retreat at the end of an exhausting day.

If anything, the view from this altitude was even more stunning, but all Domini could see were the lines of his handsome face reflected in the glass. He set her gently on the bed that had been turned down to expose powder-blue sheets, then took the rose tree from her and placed it on a highboy dresser.

"Jarod, I can't take your room." But even as she argued, he eased her out of her coat and tucked the covers around her, forcing her to sink back into the down pillows. From the corner of her eye she saw the humidifier perched on the bedside table with her note and check still taped to it.

He stood gazing down at her, legs slightly apart, hands on his hips. "You can and you will. You need privacy and the boys have been begging me to sleep in the loft with them since we moved here. I'll share their bathroom, and you'll use the one adjacent to this room. Mrs. Maughan has her suite of rooms downstairs off the hallway we passed through. Besides—" he lowered his voice "—I have another reason for wanting you in here. It's natural for you to feel an aversion to the water after what you lived through. I hope that as you look out the window day after day, you'll come to love the seascape—and not shudder like you did a few minutes ago."

She felt the tears start and turned her head away from him. "You're a very discerning man."

"My older brother lost his life out there years ago in a sailing accident," he said quietly. "I hated the very sight and smell of the Sound for months afterward, but in time I got over it. So will you."

She closed her eyes. First his brother, then his wife. Michael and Peter had come so close.

"You're exhausted. Try to sleep for a while. I'll peek in later, and if you're awake I'll let the boys come up to see you for a few minutes while you eat your dinner. I'm turning on the humidifier. Do you need help removing your robe over those stitches?"

She didn't think she could bear it if he touched her again. His very nearness made her breathless, made her heart beat uncomfortably fast. "I'd rather keep it on," she whispered hoarsely, praying he'd attribute her faltering voice to the bronchitis.

"Can I get you anything before I go downstairs? Mrs. Maughan has left ice water by the bed. The bathroom is right through the hallway here."

She finally found the courage to look up at him. "You're hovering, Doctor." A weak smile played around her lips.

His eyes actually danced. "That's part of my training, didn't you know? I'm glad to see the tears are gone. Now lie back and think of Little Miss Henny Penny."

She laughed out loud at that remark. It precipitated a cough. "Did you say that on purpose?"

"You've got to get rid of the congestion and laughter's still the best medicine I know. I'll be up later."

She turned over on her stomach to relax. For the first time in years she knew what it felt like to be cherished. *What would it be like to be his wife? To never have to say good-night or goodbye?*

Miss Henny Penny, she thought, chuckling into the pillow. Well, she could think of something a lot better than that. At some point oblivion took over, and not even the sound of the foghorns disturbed her.

CHAPTER SEVEN

MUFFLED WHISPERS and hushed voices greeted Domini's ears several hours later. She rolled over carefully and discovered three pairs of blue eyes trained expectantly on her. Unable to help herself, she let her gaze swerve to Jarod. "I think I know how Goldilocks felt. Come here, children." She held out her arms and the boys scrambled around both sides of the huge bed to hug her.

"Wrong bed, wrong hair color, but I'm not complaining." Jarod stood against the bedpost with his arms folded, bigger than life and looking pleased with the world. Domini couldn't remember seeing him in this carefree mood before. It took years off his age and gave her a glimpse of a younger Jarod, one madly in love with his wife. The image of his hands in her gilt hair, his mouth crushing hers, brought with it a sadness so intense, Domini was at a loss to understand it.

She must have communicated her distress.

"Did we hurt you, Miss Loring?" Michael sat on her lap while Peter rested on his knees next to her legs, a look of anxiety on his face.

"Would you believe that a...a safety pin in my nightgown came undone and pricked me? Of course you didn't hurt me. But I have a favor to ask both of you."

"What?" they cried out.

"Will you please call me Domini?"

The boys eyed each other, then their father. Michael spoke first. "Is it all right?" Obviously Jarod's approval was of the utmost importance.

Jarod's sweet smile made her heart turn over. "It's all right, Michael."

The little boy beamed up at Domini. "Daddy said you're too sick to read us stories tonight."

Domini wrapped her arms around him and hugged him close. "He's right. All my voice is good for right now is the tuba section." Her comment sent the boys into gales of laughter. "But I have an idea." Her eyes sparkled mischievously and commanded their attention in an instant. "I noticed the lovely stereo your father has. If you want to bring one of Children's Playhouse records in here, perhaps we could play it and you could pretend I'm talking in person. Do you know—" she tousled Michael's blond hair "—I haven't listened to one of my own recordings in years?"

"Why?" he asked in all seriousness.

"I really don't know."

"She's too busy," came the inevitable retort from Jarod, containing that tone of mockery and censure she'd learned to hate. But Michael, unaware of his father's innuendo, quickly slid off her lap.

"I'm going to get 'The Gingerbread Man.' That's my favorite. I'll be right back." He charged out the bedroom door, almost colliding with Mrs. Maughan, who was carrying Domini's dinner tray.

"Careful, Michael." Jarod immediately relieved the older woman of the tray and placed it in front of Domini.

"This looks delicious, Mrs. Maughan. Something about being away from the hospital has restored my appetite."

"I thought you'd prefer a light meal on your first night home." She smiled. "Let me know if you'd like anything else," she said over her shoulder as she went back downstairs.

Domini thought her a handsome woman with her burnished red hair swept into a chignon and her regal bearing. More important, she had a pleasant disposition and the children adored her. Jarod had referred to her as a commandant, but she must have displayed that trait only around the staff she supervised. Right now Domini thought her an angel from heaven.

The omelet tasted so delicious, Domini ate the whole thing and both pieces of toast while the boys regaled her with details of the ferry accident. Jarod excused himself because of an urgent phone call. Without his watchful presence, she could finally relax. The sweet hot tea soothed her throat, and for the first time since the accident she was beginning to feel human again.

When she found out Peter had homework, she encouraged him to do his math sitting on the bed so she could help him. Once that was finished, they put on the record and nestled down among the quilts to listen. Domini heard her own voice hit high C and wondered if she'd ever be able to do that again.

One record led to another, and after a time she noticed that both children had fallen asleep. Michael's head was burrowed against her shoulder and Peter lay spread-eagle across the foot of the bed. When Mrs. Maughan looked in, Domini waved her away, whispering to her that she wanted the boys with her a while longer, "just for this one night."

"I haven't got the heart to move them," the housekeeper whispered back. She moved about briskly, turning down lights and collecting Domini's tray. "Dr. Wolfe will see to the children later. Good night, Miss Loring. Sleep well."

Domini thanked Mrs. Maughan as she left the room. Then, feeling sleepy herself, she closed her eyes. They flew open when she heard Jarod mutter an epithet.

"This wasn't supposed to happen on your first night home, or any other night for that matter. I apologize, Domini, but I had a couple of emergencies to deal with. Where's Mrs. Maughan?" He looked out of sorts and had changed from his turtleneck to a sport shirt that was unbuttoned halfway, revealing a powerful chest, shaded by dark hair. Domini averted her eyes for fear he'd notice her staring.

"Please don't be upset with her," Domini whispered. "I persuaded her to let the boys stay a little longer. There haven't been any problems. We've all slept, actually."

He flashed her a look she couldn't decipher before he put another log on the fire. "I can see you've charmed my housekeeper just as you've charmed my children, but I won't allow this to happen again." He raked a lean hand through his hair, disheveling it. The gesture disclosed his tiredness. Busy though he was, he'd still taken the time to look after her. She almost suggested he lie down with them and rest, let her give him a back rub, the way her mother had done her father at the end of a busy day.

"Jarod." She put out a hand in appeal. "Peter needed to talk, and I believe I've convinced him to stop taking the blame for everything that happens. His eyes were as round as saucers when I told him I'd gone against your express orders so I could spend the day with them. He's thrilled to think I'm in trouble with you."

"So now you're allies, partners in crime."

A corner of her mouth lifted playfully. "Something like that, yes."

He walked to the bed and felt her forehead while he took her pulse with his other hand. "I noticed that you ate all your dinner. It's a sign that you're on the road to recovery. I won't allow the situation in my own home to set you back." His tone brooked no argument.

"I thought my presence here was meant to reassure Peter. Did I misunderstand?"

He poured distilled water into the humidifier. "No. I'm afraid the misunderstanding is all mine."

Domini stirred restlessly. "What do you mean?"

His attention fastened on Michael, who moved in his sleep to snuggle a little closer to her.

"You're no amateur actress. My apologies. Even now, knowing who you are, what you are, I'm having difficulty remembering you didn't give birth to my children."

Wounded in a manner that went beyond tears, Domini eased Michael out of her arms and turned on her side as Jarod reached for his son. Inside of a few minutes, he'd put both boys to bed.

"Good night, Domini. Sleep well."

She stared dry-eyed into the darkness. He still resented her relationship with his children. But if that was the case, why had he made things so much worse by insisting she recuperate in his own home, surrounded by his family? None of it made sense.

Was he jealous? Somehow she couldn't believe that of him. She'd observed his behavior for the past few days and could only conclude that he was a hardworking doctor and devoted father who loved his children and wanted the best for them. Jealousy wasn't an emotion she could associate with a man as stable and in charge of his destiny as Jarod.

Which left only one other possibility. Each time he watched her with the children, he suffered because she wasn't Amanda. The black-haired witch, not the golden princess, lay in his bed.

To her surprise, Domini finally went to sleep and didn't waken until Mrs. Maughan appeared with a breakfast tray. Jarod had long since left for the hospital and the children had been driven to school. Domini slept on and off during the day and listened to the radio, which demanded nothing of her. She didn't hear from the children until bedtime when they came in to talk briefly and say good-night. Mrs. Maughan remained in the room and hustled them out the door after ten minutes.

It appeared Jarod had spoken to his housekeeper and left strict instructions concerning the boys' visits. Domini realized that he had no intention of allowing his children to get too close to her. On an intellectual level she understood his reasons. But on every other level her heartache deepened.

The first day set a pattern for the next two weeks. Jarod ran his home like a hospital ward. She saw next to nothing of him except when he examined her throat and removed the stitches in her arm. He maintained a professional manner that couldn't be faulted. The memory of that one warm kiss in the emergency room, the touch of his hands on her face, might have been a dream after all.

With so many long, empty hours to fill, Domini prevailed upon Mrs. Maughan to buy her skeins of wool and some knitting patterns. She began to work secretly on Christmas stockings and handknit sweaters for Jarod and the boys. She couldn't think of a better way to keep busy and it helped pass the time. But her mind and heart dwelt constantly on Jarod and his devotion to Peter and Michael. He reserved his weekends for them and they adored him. So did she, and probably half the female population of Bremerton. If he dated other women, he kept it to himself, a fact that tortured her.

Carter phoned several times checking on her progress and asking when she'd be coming back to Seattle. She couldn't give him a date. Until Jarod pronounced her well, she had to take it a day at a time. Carter told her to mind the doctor and get better. That was all that mattered.

His attitude helped, because Jarod had pointed out some things about herself she'd taken to heart. He'd asked her about *Domini Loring, the woman.* That question had gone around in her mind for two weeks, and finally the woman in her had come to acknowledge what she yearned for above all else. Jarod's love. But if she couldn't have that, at least she could make an effort to find fulfillment outside of her career. For the first time since she could remember, she'd do something frivolous—something that had nothing to do with her career. Something just to please herself. As soon as she recovered, she'd take a long vacation.

She'd look at her life and make decisions that weren't contingent on other people's needs and desires.

On Wednesday afternoon of her third week in the Wolfe household, the sun broke through the clouds. Fresh from the shower, wearing a pink silk wrapper, Domini paused to gaze out the floor-to-ceiling window. A ferry was leaving the busy harbor. The water showed a dark green color and a flotilla of small sailboats stood out like white chalk marks on a blackboard. She no longer shuddered when she looked at the view. Jarod's specialty was family practice, but he made a superb psychiatrist.

When she heard a knock on the bedroom door she didn't interrupt her vigil as she told Mrs. Maughan to come in.

"Incredible sight, isn't it?" Jarod's entry into the bedroom was so unexpected, she could scarcely find her voice and instinctively pulled the edges of her robe closer together, afraid to turn around and face him.

"Yes. It looks like the dawn of creation the way those clouds have parted."

He stood close enough that his breath stirred the damp tendrils on her neck, and she felt light-headed at his nearness. "I never tire of the view."

She trembled. "You're never home this time of day. Is something wrong?"

"No. I'm leaving for Seattle in a few minutes and wanted to check on you first, since I won't be back until Sunday night."

The news that he'd be away for the next four days left her feeling chilled and desolate. "Do you see patients on the weekend?" she managed to ask.

"If you're talking about office visits, no. I'm taking the weekend to get my Christmas shopping done, and I don't want the boys to know about it. And while I'm gone I don't want you to think you're well enough to go exploring outside with them, even though I've given you permission to come downstairs every day."

His explanation didn't take away her sense of loss. "I want to get well as soon as possible. I'm not going to do anything foolish at this stage."

She heard his breath catch. "I realize that the enforced inactivity in a backwater like ours must be the ultimate nightmare for you, but soon—"

"Nightmare?" She rounded on him, but hadn't counted on his steadying hands. "I've loved every minute," she blurted out impetuously, aware of his eyes studying her mouth. His hands created heat where they caressed her upper arms through the thin material of her robe.

"Everyone's made me feel cherished," she whispered. "It's a wonderful feeling." She couldn't prevent the tears from glazing her eyes and he unexpectedly brushed the moist lids closed with his lips.

"That's an interesting choice of words, Domini."

She didn't try to keep the hurt out of her voice. "Mock me all you want, Jarod, since it seems to give you so much pleasure, but I meant what I said."

Her words only increased the tension between them. "You couldn't be more wrong," he said almost angrily. "Don't you know how much I want to hold you, make love to you? How much I want to kiss you...."

His confession made her dizzy with excitement, but nothing could compare to the exquisite pleasure of his mouth as it descended on hers. One hand entwined in her black curls, the other moved down her smooth back, crushing her against his chest, making it impossible to tell his heartbeat from her own. The driving force of his kiss broke down all the barriers between them, robbing her of strength so that she clung to him, and she found herself responding with a hunger she couldn't control.

Her little moaning sounds seemed to incite him. He began drinking deeply from her mouth, pressing her even closer as she wrapped her arms around his neck, wanting to give everything that had been locked inside her for so long. She couldn't tell where one kiss ended and the next began. Time had no meaning as they slowly devoured each other. He drew the very breath from her body and she gasped at the sensation of his lips against the scented hollow of her throat.

"What is it, Domini?" he whispered, burying his face in her silky hair as her body continued to tremble.

She turned her face into his shoulder. "If you kiss me any more, I think I might die of pleasure."

He groaned deeply as he cupped her flushed face in his hands. His eyes were a hot blue, incandescent as burning coal. "Do you want me to stop?" He sounded as if he'd been running a very long distance.

She turned her head to kiss his palm, unknowingly giving him her answer, for suddenly his mouth closed over hers once more and she was lost. Their hunger for each other shocked her to the very soul. This was no bland embrace, no mere solace. Jarod seemed as consumed by the fire that blazed between them as she was. She'd never experienced anything with which to compare this sweet, wild ecstasy that permeated her heart and body. She loved Jarod to the depth of her being and couldn't prevent herself from showing him that he was life itself to her. No kiss was long enough, deep enough.

"Daddy's home!" Michael's excited voice floated up the staircase into the bedroom. At the sound of his voice, Domini started to come to her senses and tried to break their kiss, but Jarod moaned his displeasure and held her trapped in his strong arms. The patter of feet in the hall made her panic and she pushed against his chest, forcing him to relinquish his hold. She tore her lips from his as Michael came running into the bedroom with Peter not far behind.

"Daddy! What are you doing?" The little boy stood staring at the two of them. Jarod's hands slid reluctantly from her body, finally allowing her to escape to the bathroom where she could dress in privacy and try to recover from the onslaught of his demands.

"I was kissing her, Michael."

Domini could hear their conversation through the door as she clutched the sink with both hands, waiting for the throbbing of her pulse to subside. She marveled that Jarod could sound so reasonable when they'd both gone far beyond the point of coherent thought. If the children hadn't arrived when they did, she could never have denied him.

She looked in the mirror and a different woman stared back, one with her hair in wanton disarray, a rosy flush on her throat and cheeks, a mouth swollen from ardent lovemaking.

Their voices faded as she took her time getting dressed; she needed time to pull herself together. When she emerged from the bathroom dressed in wool pants and a blouse, Jarod was nowhere to be found, but the children were waiting for her in the bedroom. Their sober expressions troubled her.

"Domini? Now that Daddy's gone, can we talk to you for a minute?"

"Of course. Come and sit." She patted a spot next to her on the bed. Michael scrambled into her arms but Peter remained standing in much the same way his father did when he had something important on his mind.

"Were you kissing Daddy goodbye?" Michael piped up earnestly.

Domini bowed her head, hoping for inspiration. "Is that what he told you?"

"Daddy said it was none of our business, but we think you're going away," Peter said in solemn tones.

"Children—" Her voice caught. "I'm not going anywhere until your father says I'm well enough."

"Then we don't want you to ever get better," Michael asserted and pressed his head against her shoulder.

"Did you kiss him because you love him?"

Peter's persistence caught her offguard. "I care about all of you," she murmured and slid off the bed, grasping both their hands. "And while he's away, I think this would be the perfect time to make some plans for Christmas. It's only twelve days away." Michael's attention was easily diverted, but Peter had a stubborn streak like his father.

"Are you going to be here for Christmas?"

Domini smiled at Peter. "I wouldn't want to be any place else." It was an answer of sorts, and because it was so obviously the truth, Peter seemed mollified. "I didn't see a Christmas tree when I went downstairs earlier," she went on. "What are your plans, or do you know?"

Michael shrugged his shoulders. "Daddy said he's been too busy, but that he'll get one when he comes back from Seattle."

"Well—" Domini rolled her eyes in exaggerated fashion "—I have a wonderful idea. Why don't we order a tree since I can't go outside? We'll have it delivered and we'll get it all decorated so when your daddy comes home, it'll be the first thing he sees when he walks in the living room."

"Goody!" Michael cried out. "Let's put it in front of the big window."

"I know where we keep the lights and stuff," Peter offered, starting to get into the spirit of things.

"Good. And when we've finished the tree, we can make Christmas candy. And then we'll talk about what we're going to buy your daddy and Mrs. Maughan for Christmas. I think I remember how to make giant gingerbread men, too—we can write out the names in frosting and deliver the cookies to all your friends for the holidays." Her suggestion produced cries of joy. The boys chattered all the way downstairs as they made their way to the kitchen where Mrs. Maughan was busy preparing their evening meal.

Before Domini could open her mouth, the children had told the older woman everything. She beamed. "I know a place to phone that delivers trees. Do you want a flocked one?"

"No," Peter responded decisively. "Daddy says he likes the green ones best."

"Make it *real* tall," Michael added.

"If you'll make the call," Domini muttered to Mrs. Maughan, "I'll get the Christmas decorations out of storage. The boys can help me."

She nodded. "They're in boxes out in the garage on the shelves along the west wall. I'm afraid they're not much, Domini. Feel free to do whatever you want with them."

"Thank you, Mrs. Maughan. It's been years since I've gone to any trouble for Christmas. Children make all the difference."

"You can say that again," she said chuckling softly.

"Phone right now," the boys pleaded. "Maybe they'll bring it tonight! Please?"

"Even if they do, we'll have to wait until tomorrow night to decorate because you've got school in the morning. Now why don't you wash your hands while I call about the tree. Then we'll eat dinner."

With shouts of excitement, the boys did her bidding. But their faces fell when they assembled for dinner, because Mrs. Maughan announced that the tree couldn't be delivered until morning. Domini suggested they get the decorations out and see what they had to work with before going to bed.

The three boxes contained white lights, red satin balls, a wreath for the front door and a nativity scene. It was a start, but Domini had a dozen ideas she wanted to carry out; she'd have to wait until morning to work on them.

The boys went willingly upstairs to take their baths and get ready for bed when Domini promised to tell them a story before they fell asleep. It took three stories before she could tiptoe from the loft and go to bed herself. But after tossing and turning for a quarter of an hour, she got up and wandered over to the window. Everything in Domini cried out to reassure the boys that if it were up to her, she'd stay forever. She couldn't love them more if they were her own children. But until she saw Jarod again and he could admit that the passion they'd shared had been no temporary assuagement of appetite, she had to remain silent.

Jarod wasn't the kind of man to make love to a woman if he didn't have feelings for her. She felt sure of that. At least she had the satisfaction of knowing Jarod desired her. But she wanted him to love her. She would have to wait until Sunday for a sign that he couldn't live without her either.

Finally her eyelids grew heavy and she went back to bed, wondering if Jarod was in bed, too, and if his sleep was as restless as hers. She hoped their interlude had given him permanent insomnia.

She awakened the next morning bright and early and went downstairs to help Mrs. Maughan get the children off to school, promising them they'd spend their Friday night making the house look beautiful for Christmas.

Thankful to be allowed downstairs after her illness, Domini talked Mrs. Maughan into letting her do small tasks around the house. As they worked, she told the housekeeper of her plans to decorate, insisting that she wanted to pay for everything. It would be her way of saying thank-you to the entire family.

Mrs. Maughan acted delighted by the whole idea, and on Domini's instructions, went into town to purchase enough multicolored lights and Scandinavian wooden ornaments to cover the fifteen-foot noble fir that was delivered. While the housekeeper was out, Domini made gingerbread cookies, then set them aside for the boys to decorate. The smaller ones they could hang on the tree; the others they could give to their friends. She planned a real "Nutcracker" Christmas for them, complete with toy soldiers and sugarplum fairies.

On a burst of inspiration, Domini phoned the florist and ordered six red poinsettias, some smilax and holly for the stair railing and mantel, and an enormous blue hydrangea for the coffee table. She also bought a manger scene made out of candles, which they could light on Christmas Eve. And she couldn't resist a sprig of mistletoe for the front hallway.

Domini put everything on her bank card; she'd reimburse Mrs. Maughan with her travelers' checks. Domini couldn't remember the last time she'd splurged like this for any reason, but right now she wanted to create a fantasy Christmas none of them would forget.

Domini hurried excitedly upstairs and pulled from under Jarod's bed the stockings she'd made during her convalescence. She had finished the Scandinavian-style sweaters for the boys, but was still working on the yoke for Jarod's. In another few days, it would be ready, and she'd ask Mrs. Maughan to take it to the shop to be sewn together and blocked.

When Mrs. Maughan arrived from town, Domini had hung the stockings on the mantel. Tears gathered in the housekeeper's eyes when she saw the stocking Domini had made for her. "It's beautiful," she said in awe, putting down the packages. "I can't believe you made these."

"I learned to sew and knit from my mother long before I did much of anything else."

The older woman stared at Domini for several seconds. "You're a wonder. Already you've transformed this house."

Domini smiled. "*You're* the wonder, Mrs. Maughan. You've made a home for this family. Jarod was blessed to have found you, and I happen to know the children love you. I don't know if I've told you this or not, but when Peter wrote that letter, he asked if you could come to the studio, too."

Her eyes filled to overflowing. "No, I didn't know. Thank you for telling me that." She sniffed. "I'd just better go fix my face. It's time to pick up the children."

Mrs. Maughan's departure coincided with the florist's delivery and soon the house looked like a Christmas card. The fresh greenery and flowers combined with the smell of spicy gingerbread, adding to the children's enchantment as they raced through the front door to the living room, calling Domini's name. All her work so far was worth it, just to see the wonder on their faces.

They shrieked in delight at the sight of the huge red felt stockings depicting a brown-and-white gingerbread man for Michael, a jeweled blue fox for Peter. The pastel Mother Goose for Mrs. Maughan and the mighty sailor man for Jarod, done in blue and white crystal beads and sequins, drew equal shouts of joy. Then the boys ran to inspect everything else, examining all the new ornaments and choosing their own favorites to hang on the tree.

Peter went out to the garage and brought in the stepladder. Domini eyed it doubtfully. They'd need someone taller than she or Mrs. Maughan to decorate the very top of the tree. But they started stringing lights from the bottom and worked up as far as they could reach.

"I'll call a friend who lives in town and see if he'll come over later on," Mrs. Maughan announced. "Why don't we all stop and have an early dinner while we wait for him?"

Domini agreed. "We have plenty of other things to do," she said cheerfully as they went into the kitchen.

"Peter? Look at all those cookies!" Michael whispered in awe. Each one had a red ribbon run through a hole at the top.

"After we eat, we can begin decorating them to hang on the tree. The larger cookies are for your friends."

The boys ate dinner in record time so they could set to work creating their individual masterpieces with icing, sprinkles and glitter. There were plenty of mishaps and several cookies found their way into tummies, but on the whole, the cookie production was a huge success.

"I hope you saved some for me. I'm starving." Domini froze as she heard the familiar male voice.

Her heart began to hammer painfully in her chest as she and the children whirled around to see Jarod standing there in his overcoat, hair still damp from the light rain outside. "Dad! Look what Domini's made!" they cried out and ran over to him to exhibit their handiwork.

"You can have this one," Michael offered magnanimously, and Jarod promptly devoured it, flicking his gaze in her direction at last.

She dusted the flour from her hands. "I—we thought you weren't coming home until Sunday."

"I thought so, too," he murmured. His eyes were everywhere, warm and searching, the way they'd been yesterday afternoon, when he'd come to the bedroom. "The aroma of fresh gingerbread must be the reason I drove all the way home, even though I should've stayed in Seattle."

"It's a good thing you did, Dad. We need you to put the lights on the top of the Christmas tree. Mrs. Maughan was going to get Mr. Lawson to do it," said Peter.

"I'll just call him back and tell him not to bother." Mrs. Maughan hurried into the study.

"Daddy? Did you see the stockings Domini made for us?" By this time Michael was in his father's arms, patting his cheeks.

"I saw everything, Mike, and I thought that I'd returned to Santa's workshop. It looks like some elves have been very busy."

Michael laughed happily. "Domini's not an elf, Daddy. You're silly."

Startling blue eyes swept over Domini. "No, you're right, Mike. There's nothing elfish about Domini, but you have to admit there's a magic to everything she does." His words should have suffused her with joy, but his eyes looked puzzled, even haunted. "Let me grab a bite to eat and I'll tackle the lights."

"Hooray!" the boys cheered, following their father into the hall to hang up his coat, chattering about the wooden ornaments they'd saved for him to put on the tree. Jarod then presented them with a new recording of *The Messiah*. The heavenly music soon filled the house with the joy of Christmas. And it filled Domini's heart, as well.

While she cleaned up the cookie mess, she felt Jarod's penetrating glance on her as Mrs. Maughan served him his dinner. His eyes always seemed to be asking a question—one she had no idea how to answer. It cast a pall on the night's festivities.

Mrs. Maughan finally disappeared from the kitchen and Jarod got up from the table, gathering up the last of the dishes. Without conscious thought, Domini rinsed them and put them in the dishwasher.

"Tell me something, Domini," he murmured. "Does Christmas always bring out your domestic instincts? Or is this a momentary aberration?"

CHAPTER EIGHT

"AN ABERRATION, of course," she said, trying to continue the joke that wasn't really a joke. Obviously, he still assumed that her career was the only thing she took seriously. But then another thought occurred to her and she slowly turned to face him, her back pressed against the counter. "Are you trying to tell me I've overstepped the bounds in your home?"

"Of course not," he said almost angrily.

"I'm sorry," she went on as if he hadn't spoken. "After being waited on for weeks, I felt it was my turn to do something to show my gratitude. But apparently I've offended you and outstayed my welcome. Under the circumstances I think it's best if I plan to leave in the morning."

Jarod started to say something but was interrupted by Peter. "You said you were going to spend Christmas with us!" he accused from the doorway, his expression devoid of animation as he looked from Domini to Jarod's ashen face. No telling how long he'd been standing there listening. She heard Jarod suck in his breath.

"It's not polite to eavesdrop, Peter." Jarod tugged at his tie to loosen it. "Sometimes grown-ups have misunderstandings—just like you and Mike have—but then you sort things out. For your information, Domini's not going anywhere yet. She's still not completely recovered from the bronchitis. Now I think you ought to apologize to her for the intrusion.''

Peter's face crumpled as he ran to her and threw his arms around her in a fierce hug. "I'm sorry, Domini. I love you."

Domini hugged him back. "I love you, too, darling."

Jarod's face wore a brooding expression. "Domini and I will be out in a minute, Peter," he began, but Peter ran from the kitchen without looking at his father.

It pained Domini to think she was the reason for their estrangement. She gasped softly when she felt Jarod's hands on her shoulders, kneading with gentle pressure. "I'm sorry, too," he whispered in a husky voice. "I offended *you*, when in my clumsy way I meant to compliment you for bringing the spirit of Christmas back into this house. You must have spent hours working on those stockings. There's nothing momentary about a project like that. I suppose I'm still finding it difficult to reconcile the celebrity with the warm and caring woman my children adore. Forgive me?" By this time he had moved around to cradle her flushed face in his hands.

Domini lifted troubled green eyes to his. "Of course I forgive you, but why is it so difficult to...to see me working in your kitchen or doing things for the boys?" She felt that finally she was getting closer to understanding this complex man.

His head lowered. "Right now I can't think why, because I need to kiss you too badly. You didn't have to put up mistletoe. Why do you suppose I didn't get any sleep last night? And why do you think I came

back home as soon as I could manage it, if not to finish what we started in my bedroom?''

His mouth descended on hers without giving her a
chance to say anything else and once more she was
caught in a world where coherent thought ceased and
only sensual need remained. She'd been aching for this
rapture since yesterday, had dreamed about it, but
now Jarod's lovemaking was starting a new fire that
made her forget where they were.

''He's kissing her again,'' Michael murmured from
a crack in the doorway. Jarod must have noticed the
resignation in his son's voice because he broke their
kiss and moved away, taking a deep breath as he ran
shaky hands through his hair.

Domini turned to grasp the counter for support. She
wasn't prepared for this abrupt descent back to reality. She doubted she could walk even a few steps the
way she was feeling right now. Unbelievably, she felt
his arms slide around her from behind. ''Do you have
any idea how much I want you?'' he whispered. For a
moment they simply stood together, relishing the
closeness of their bodies. It took a knock on the
kitchen door to finally effect a separation.

''I'm coming, Mike,'' he said on a low groan.
Domini didn't dare look at him for fear she wouldn't
be able to let him go. Her desire for Jarod had trans-
ferred itself into actual pain that only his lovemaking
could relieve. It was agony to pull away.

When she joined the family in the living room a few
minutes later, she marveled at Jarod's ability to act as
if nothing momentous had happened between them,
and she tried to behave in an equally nonchalant
manner. But nothing escaped Jarod's keen eye. Once
or twice during the decorating of the tree he gave her

a secret smile that sent her pulses racing. Each time she had to look away, knowing hectic color filled her cheeks.

"It's beautiful," the children murmured, as they stood back to survey their work. Jarod had turned off all the lights, and the tree shone bright in the darkness; Domini had to admit the room looked like fairyland.

Jarod cleared his throat. His eyes glowed with a brilliance that matched his children's. "Is your voice strong enough to sing 'Silent Night' for us, Domini?"

"Why don't I sing a verse and then you all join in?" Jarod nodded slowly and without a word they all clasped hands. Choosing a key in a lower register than usual, Domini began to sing. And to her joy, her voice rang out pure and true. Though it didn't sound as powerful as before, that was because she didn't want to strain it. She expected the others to take up the next verse but to her astonishment, they simply stared at her.

"Will you sing the rest?" Peter asked quietly.

"Please," Michael chimed in.

Not daring to look Jarod's way, she sang the second and third verses, then urged them to sing the first verse with her again. The sound of their voices thrilled her.

"Sing 'The Night before Christmas'!" the boys begged when they'd finished.

"How does your throat feel?" Jarod questioned, once again the concerned doctor.

"If you want to know the truth, I feel wonderful," Domini confessed. "I can't believe I was ever all that sick, thanks to you."

Jarod appeared to digest her words and looked down at the boys. "If I let her sing one more song, you have to promise to go straight to bed afterwards." The boys nodded and sat down on the couch with their father to listen.

"I really need a piano for this song." She smiled. "Feel free to add any sound effects along the way." With that encouragement, she began the rendition favored by children on her hospital tours over the past few years. Still, she suspected that she'd never given a more professional performance than she did now.

The boys grew quiet, but they soon started to giggle. She acted her way through the song and everyone joined in to sing, "Merry Christmas to all, and to all a good-night." As her voice faded the boys leaped from the couch and ran to hug her. After more kisses, Jarod urged them upstairs and told Domini to stay put. He'd be back down shortly.

In her dreamy, euphoric state, Domini curled up on the couch and stared at the Christmas tree lights, thinking she'd never been so happy. But the ringing of the telephone shattered her bliss. A call in Jarod's home usually meant an emergency of some kind. Her disappointment was more than she could believe when she saw the withdrawn look on his face as he entered the living room.

"You're wanted on the phone, Domini. It's Carter Phillips. Since I know you have a lot to talk about, I'll go to the hospital— I need to check on a newborn with jaundice. I should have driven over earlier as it is."

"Jarod?" Her voice faltered as she followed him to the front door. "Shall I wait up for you?"

A nerve hammered along his jaw as he put on his overcoat. "If I'm not home within a half hour, you'll

know there were complications," he stated, effectively shutting her out.

But Domini wasn't about to let him leave like this
when she knew their evening might have ended very
differently if Carter hadn't phoned at such an inop-
portune moment. "I'm used to complications. I'm a
doctor's daughter, remember?" She took a deep
breath. "I'll be up when you come back."

His brooding eyes regarded her for a long moment.
"Do you think you should keep Phillips waiting when
it's long distance?" He buttoned his coat. "Good
night, Domini."

"Good night," she murmured, half sobbing as she
heard the click of the front door. The finality of that
sound forced Domini to face the inescapable fact that
Jarod had no intention of returning early so they could
pick up where they'd left off.

She picked up the receiver in the kitchen to talk to
Carter, and it took all her control to act as if nothing
had happened. He wanted to know how she was progressing and told her not to worry about the programs. They'd taped far enough ahead to cover her for
another two weeks. After that they could show a few
reruns, if necessary. He passed along news and messages and sent get-well wishes from everyone at the
studio before he finally said good-night.

Domini stayed up for another hour after talking to
Carter, praying she'd hear Jarod's car in the drive-
way. She finally gave up the vigil, turned off the
Christmas tree lights and went to bed.

Even then, she listened for Jarod's return, wondering why Carter's phone call should create such a
change in Jarod's behavior. Just when she thought
they'd reached a turning point in their relationship,

he'd again become the implacable man who'd charged into her office that morning, demanding satisfaction for alleged injuries.

She tossed and turned half the night, anxious for morning to come so she could talk to Jarod. But by accident or design, there never seemed to be a moment when they were alone.

He walked in on her and the children Saturday evening as they watched her television show. He stared at her with an unfathomable look in his eyes and then disappeared into his study for the rest of the night. She'd imagined he'd been out Christmas shopping, but if that was true, it hadn't done anything to improve his mood.

The week before Christmas started just like all the others. The children went to school and Jarod went to the clinic. The only difference was Domini's condition; she felt totally recovered except for occasional congestion. She was anxious to keep busy, helping Mrs. Maughan with the household chores. These weeks had opened up a new world to Domini and she could no longer imagine living without Jarod and the children. Yet she'd have to go back to work one day soon. She panicked at the thought that Jarod didn't feel the same way she did and would let her go when the time came.

Domini looked forward to Thursday when the children would be home for the holiday. But to her chagrin, they'd been invited to a birthday party sleepover. Jarod was still in Seattle, having driven there on Tuesday. Just when she would have relished a houseful of company, everyone had gone. Under the circumstances, Domini felt it ridiculous for Mrs.

Maughan to remain at the house and urged her to go to her daughter's.

After some friendly argument, Mrs. Maughan finally agreed to go, promising to return the following afternoon. On her way there, she kindly agreed to take the sweater Domini had finished for Jarod to the shop to be blocked. As soon as she'd gone, Domini turned on a live broadcast of *Rigoletto* and washed her hair in the kitchen sink. When it was dry, she combed the curls and realized her hair had grown longer during her convalescence. A glance in the mirror showed her that it tumbled past her shoulders now, glistening and unrestrained.

Her jeans fit a little more loosely, but the weight loss was slight—Mrs. Maughan had seen to that. After slipping into a comfortable yellow cotton sweater Domini curled up on the couch to read a thriller while she finished listening to the opera, but she couldn't concentrate. Jarod was purposely staying away. He regretted making love to her, it seemed, so he'd taken measures to ensure that he would never again be carried away by the passion of the moment. To him, that was evidently all it was. Tears trickled down her cheeks.

She put down her book and stared into the growing darkness with a heavy heart. Some part of Jarod didn't like Domini, and another part still loved his wife—a fatal combination. Domini decided she had no choice but to leave Bremerton the day after Christmas, whether she still had any symptoms or not.

The hours passed with agonizing slowness. At ten, Domini turned off the television and went upstairs, bitterly disappointed that the one night they could have been alone—to talk, at least—Jarod had chosen to be away.

The moon shone cold and clear, casting its reflection on the darkened water. The sight was so unexpected after weeks of fog, so mystical, that Domini paused at the loft window to absorb the view. Twinkling lights indicated activity out in the harbor, and faint ship noises reached her, even at this distance. Unable to tear herself away, Domini sank down on the lower bunk of the boys' bed to watch and listen to the sounds of the night. At some point her eyelids grew heavy and she fell back against the mattress into a deep sleep.

Later that night something wakened her, and she sat up with a start. Jarod was calling her name. She heard footsteps dashing up the stairs. Without her watch, she had no idea what time it was, but apparently he'd decided to come back from Seattle without telling anyone.

"Jarod?" She hastened to let him know she was in the house. She'd heard genuine alarm in his voice when he called her name. Sliding quickly down from the bunk bed, she turned toward the hall. Jarod must have seen the movement out of the corner of his eye because he left his bedroom on a run and came to an abrupt halt in the loft.

"Domini?" he said in a disbelieving tone.

A shaft of light from the hallway fell across the open space between them, revealing her body to his gaze. "What's wrong?" Her voice was still husky from sleep. She smoothed back a strand of tousled hair from her flushed cheek.

His eyes moved slowly to her throat and then her shoulder, partially exposed by the wrinkled sweater.

"When I couldn't find you, I thought you'd gone," he murmured thickly.

She took a step forward. "You mean, back to Seattle?"

He nodded, as if in shock. "Then when I saw your things still in the bedroom, I thought you might have gone out walking because it's such a beautiful night. Even worse, I had this vision of you trying to make your way down to the boat house in the dark and fal—" he broke off talking.

Domini searched his tall, lean frame but his features were indistinct with the light at his back. A moment before, he'd sounded almost frantic; his apparent worry made no sense, considering that he'd purposely stayed away from her since the weekend. "I fell asleep looking at the lights on the bay."

"It didn't occur to me that you'd be in *here*."

He sounded so strange. Did he think she was trying to waylay him? "I-I had no idea you were coming back tonight. I was drawn to the view on my way up to bed. Since the children were sleeping over at a friend's—"

"Domini—" His voice was rough, almost harsh. "You don't have to explain anything to me." An odd intensity radiated between them. They were talking on one level, but she was conscious of some deeper emotion emanating from him.

"Do you have any idea how beautiful you are?" he demanded. "I've gone out of my mind wondering how to stay away from you now that you're well again, but a man can only take so much. I don't know how to fight it anymore. Help me," he asked raggedly.

Help you. She mouthed the words, too entranced by his admission to grasp what he was asking. "Do you want me to go?'' she questioned softly, trying to keep the tremor out of her voice.

He shook his head hopelessly. "You don't understand. I don't want you going anywhere. I want to touch you again, but if I do, I won't be able to stop and there are too many reasons why I can't let that happen.''

Now what was he saying? "Is it something I've done?'' She took a step forward, beseeching him with her eyes. "Does this have to do with the children?''

"Domini . . .'' Her name came out a tortured whisper. "Phillips has this—''

"Carter?'' she cried out, interrupting him. "What does he have to do with us?''

His expression was grim. "Not *us*. You!''

"What are you getting at?''

He shifted his stance. "He manipulates you, Domini. How long did you say you've been with Phillips? Eight years? Your first and only employer? You'd do anything for him.''

She blinked in astonishment. "You couldn't be more wrong.''

After a brief silence he said, "It's my experience that most people don't know when they're being manipulated. He hired you at an impressionable, vulnerable nineteen years of age and molded you into the star you are today. He uses your gratitude as leverage to get his way, and he's so clever that you look upon him as your benefactor.''

She tossed her head indignantly, unable to credit what she was hearing. "You don't know what you're saying. I've been extremely happy at Children's Playhouse—exactly because he *isn't* the kind of dictator you're describing.''

He gave her a condescending smile. "Then how do you explain the contest?"

"What do you mean?"

"You told me you didn't approve of it on principle. Yet you did it for Phillips."

"I don't like contests that bring the public inside the studio. I prefer to keep my distance so I can enjoy what little private life I have, but I was willing to try it once. If I'd really put up a protest, Carter would never have forced me to do it."

He studied her pensively. "That's the point, Domini. You didn't protest because deep down you didn't want to go against Phillips." He crossed his arms. "Even in the emergency room at the hospital when you'd barely arrived—suffering from hypothermia, an injured arm, not to mention bronchitis—you were thinking about Phillips! You were worrying about that blasted job instead of taking care of yourself."

Hot color rose to her cheeks. "Are you trying to tell me, *Dr. Wolfe*, that if you'd been in my place after the accident, you wouldn't have wanted the clinic or the hospital to know of your whereabouts?" She shook her head in exasperation. "And as for this supposed hold Carter has over me, let me make something perfectly clear. I didn't protest the contest because I didn't feel that strongly about it! Period!

"You may have studied psychology at medical school, Jarod, but it seems you missed out on one important fact. Some people do things for the sheer joy of doing them! You don't need to dig into my deep, dark subconscious, to find motives for what I do. I like my job! At times I even love it! Music's my life!"

A nerve pulsed along his jaw. "I stand corrected. But your words have proved to me that my reasons for not getting involved are valid. It would be futile to discuss them."

If he'd slapped her face, he couldn't have made it clearer that he could never love her. The finality of his voice devastated her. "Will you tell the children that I'm well enough to go back to work? I promised Peter I wouldn't leave until you gave your permission. I think it would be best if I left first thing in the morning." She hurried past him.

"Domini . . ." He followed her to the stairs. Maybe it was a trick of light, but she thought his face was strangely pale. "Don't go till after Christmas. I'll stay out of your way."

Didn't he know that spending Christmas with him and the boys, only to leave immediately afterward would only prolong the pain? "The longer I stay, the harder it will be on everyone. Peter's suspected all along that I might go. It won't surprise him or Michael."

He stood on the landing, his legs slightly apart, as if he were readying himself for a struggle. "Then you're really going?" They faced each other like adversaries.

Everything in Domini cried out to Jarod to stop her. He had only to say the words, but in their place was the hateful silence that smothered all her hopes and dreams. "Yes. Now if you'll excuse me, I need to start packing."

His mouth had thinned to a white line. "There'll be a scene with the boys no matter how it's handled, but I honestly believe it will be easier on them if we drive you home to Mercer Island in the morning. I'll explain that you have work commitments."

Although it was on the tip of her tongue to tell him she'd make her own arrangements, she had second thoughts as she considered his suggestion. The parting with the boys would be painful, though less traumatic perhaps, if they could be with their father on the ride back to Bremerton. Driving away from the cliff house, waving to them through the car window would be too cruel. "I think that's probably the best idea," she muttered, dashing up the stairs to the bedroom.

Domini needed to channel her energy into something physical and immediately began her packing. She didn't break down until her hands caressed the lace-and-satin bed jacket Jarod and the children had given her for a get-well present. She lay down on the bed and buried her face in it as great, heaving sobs racked her body. At some point during the night, she fell into an exhausted sleep.

Domini awakened at dawn to the sound of a foghorn and stumbled from the bed to shower. She made up her face to disguise all vestiges of tears, then dressed in the same outfit she'd worn when they met for dinner at the Coast Inn.

The house was quiet as she crept down the stairs with her bags, past the loft where she presumed Jarod slept. She never knew if he was home or not because of the emergencies that frequently got him out of bed.

She poured herself some juice and sat down at the kitchen table to write a thank-you letter to Mrs. Maughan. The woman was a saint in Domini's eyes. She ran Jarod's home so beautifully and took perfect care of his children. Domini's hand shook as she signed her name. She slipped the letter in an envelope and left it on the table where Mrs. Maughan would be sure to find it.

With that accomplished, Domini went upstairs one more time to get all the packages she'd wrapped and put them under the Christmas tree. Jarod's gift wouldn't be ready for another few days. Mrs. Maughan would have to see to it.

"I didn't think you'd be up yet."

Domini hadn't heard Jarod come down the stairs. He was showered, shaved and dressed in gray trousers and a black pullover. And he'd never looked more appealing, more attractive. His drawn, shadowed face only added to his male beauty.

"I had a lot to do and I wanted to be ready on time."

Jarod moved closer, studying her thoroughly, almost impersonally. "I thought I'd seen every shade of green reflecting off the Sound, but your eyes defy description." He sighed, running a hand through his hair. "You don't look like the same person I met at the studio. The rest and relaxation have made all the difference. Don't let that change. I realize you're anxious to go back to your old life, but don't push it, Domini. You could have a relapse if you try to keep up your earlier pace."

His concern appeared to be purely professional, and this plunged the dagger a little deeper. She'd half turned to leave when his hands suddenly descended on her shoulders and prevented her from escaping. "Promise me you'll slow down, that you'll take better care of yourself."

His nearness, the warmth of his fingers, seemed to rob her of coherent thought.

"Domini?" He shook her gently, but she couldn't remember what they were talking about. Suddenly nothing seemed more important than touching him.

But he didn't want that. He didn't want anything from her.

"Let me go, Jarod."

Their faces were so close she could see the throbbing of a nerve along his jawline. He stared at her through glazed eyes, then pivoted suddenly away.

"I'll load everything in the car and go for the children. I should be back within ten minutes." He strode from the living room as if he couldn't get away from her fast enough.

Domini braced herself against the table in an effort to recover. She'd been all right until he touched her. Like a match to tinder, the sensations he created had kindled a fire inside her. She was glad to be leaving, she told herself fiercely. Glad he could never make her feel this way again.

With her rose tree in one arm and her purse in the other, she started down the hall and almost collided with Michael, who came flying through the front door.

"Domini!" He wrapped his arms around her waist. "Don't leave. Don't go."

"Michael! Go out to the car, son," Jarod ordered from the doorway. A dull red flush stained his cheeks.

"No!" Michael continued to clutch at her dress, ignoring his father's command.

"What did you say to me?" he asked in a deceptively quiet voice.

"I don't want Domini to go back to Seattle, Daddy. Peter says it's your fault she's leaving," he shouted as the tears poured down his pale face.

"It's no one's fault, darling," Domini intervened. "Do you remember my boss, Mr. Phillips?" Michael nodded. "Well, he phoned last night to find out if I was well enough to entertain some sick children in hospitals like I did last year," she lied. "Remember?" He nodded unwillingly. "Your daddy says I'm much better now, so when I thought about all those sick little patients who need cheering up at Christmas time, I couldn't disappoint them."

Michael blinked, assimilating what she'd said. "But we want you to be home with us, don't we, Daddy?"

"I'd like that, too, Michael," she plunged in once more. "What if I phone you Christmas morning, after you've opened all your presents?"

"Do you promise?" he asked in such solemn tones she wanted to weep.

"Yes, I promise," she said, her voice quavering.

"Now I'd like you to apologize to Domini and me," Jarod said, not unkindly. He crouched to take the boy in his arms. Michael crept into them, sobbing his heart out. When the storm subsided, he lifted his head from his father's broad shoulder and gazed up at Domini, his eyes like two drenched cornflowers.

"I'm sorry, Domini. I'm sorry, Daddy."

"That sounds better," Jarod murmured, kissing the top of the boy's head.

"Can I sit with Domini when we drive her back to Seattle?"

Wordlessly Domini sought Jarod's approval, which he gave with a slight nod of his dark head. "Why don't we ride in the back seat where there's plenty of room? I've made something good for us to eat when we get hungry. We can read stories and play some games. Shall we try to beat Peter and your father at Twenty Questions?"

"Peter's not coming," Michael said in a forlorn little voice. His father straightened and swung him into his arms, holding him close for a moment. Then he set Michael down.

"What happened to Peter?" Domini whispered anxiously as Jarod helped her into the back seat of the car, relieving her of the tree.

His face darkened. "You don't really need me to answer that, do you?" He shut the door and went around to his side of the car, depositing the tree on the floor beside him.

Their eyes met through the rearview mirror. "Jarod, there must be something you can do."

"I'm taking you home. When I get back will be soon enough to start picking up the pieces."

"What pieces?" Michael questioned, looking from one to the other.

"It means that after we drop Domini off, we're going to get Peter and start enjoying our Christmas holiday." They turned onto the coastal highway.

"Will you come and see us after Christmas?" Michael beseeched her.

"She can't, Michael, because she's going to do another tour," Jarod answered before she had a chance to speak.

Domini stared out the window as the black Mercedes sped toward Seattle, hardly aware of the lovely weather.

"Why do you have to go, Domini?"

Again, Jarod took over. "She's the Story Princess. Remember how you couldn't wait to meet her? Well, there are thousands of children in eastern Washington who love her, too, and can't wait to see her in person."

Michael's round blue eyes studied Domini so intensely, she turned her head and smiled at him.

"But you're not really a princess," he said.

Domini didn't dare look at Jarod just then. "No. I'm an ordinary person who goes to work. Just like your father."

"But if you go away, you won't be on TV anymore."

"Yes I will, Michael. Remember when you were at the studio? They tape several shows at one time so that even when I'm gone, there's a program to play."

He cuddled up next to her and rested his head against her arm. "But you won't really be there. It won't be the same."

She closed her eyes. "If you mean I won't be at the studio, then you're right."

"Do you like being the Story Princess?" he asked in a sleepy voice.

"She loves it, Michael. It's her life!" Jarod answered, and the bitterness in his voice was unmistakable.

"Oh..." was all he said as his eyelids closed. Domini could scarcely breathe as she saw two tears slip out from his lashes and trickle down his cheeks.

The rest of the journey was made in agonizing silence. Michael fell into a deep sleep; he probably hadn't slept much the night before, she thought, stroking his fine, blond hair.

Without preliminary, Jarod took her bags and tree from the car as soon as they pulled up in front of her building. Domini eased away from Michael and left him lying on the back seat. She hurried to the front door, key in hand. Jarod couldn't wait to be rid of her and she had no desire to prolong the inevitable.

"No—I don't need your help," she insisted when Jarod would have carried her bags inside. "Hurry back to the car before Michael wakes up.'' She inserted her key in the lock and pushed the front door open, shoving her bags inside.

"Domini—"

"Goodbye, Jarod." She hugged the tree to her breast, needing something to hold on to. "Thank you for everything. It sounds inadequate, I know, but I mean it sincerely."

His handsome face seemed a distorted version of itself and his beautiful blue eyes were hooded. "I wish the Story Princess a long and healthy reign—please believe that." He put some gift-wrapped packages from him and the children on the floor beside her bags. "Goodbye, Domini."

CHAPTER NINE

"HAPPY NEW YEAR, Carter—even if it is almost February!"

"Dom! You're back!" Carter leaped out of his swivel chair and crossed the room to hug her. "Let me look at you." His piercing black eyes took swift inventory. "When I saw you at Christmas, you were too pale. But now you're tanned to perfection and I like your hair longer. But why do I have the feeling you're not on top of the world?"

"Of course I am, silly."

"Wasn't Hawaii up to your expectations?"

"I had a marvelous time."

He shook his head. "It's your eyes. There's a sadness.... Want to tell me about it?"

"No. But I'd like to discuss my schedule with you."

He whistled in relief. "I thought you were going to tell me you were resigning. Sit down. Let's talk."

Domini took a chair opposite his desk. "First, I want to thank you for giving me a leave of absence. I needed that month on the beach. I saw a doctor this morning. He took an X ray and said it revealed a perfectly healthy set of lungs. I'm completely recovered from the bronchitis."

"Excellent." Carter fingered his mustache. "You know, Dom, I've warned you for several years that you need to take a vacation from this place like the others do. The three weeks you took to be with your father at the end don't count. Are you finally convinced that a rest from work is necessary to your well-being?''

"I know you're right but I've never liked traveling on my own. When I was little I went with my parents, and Father took me on a lot of trips after Mother's death. But when he died, I hated the idea of going off alone. However, this bout of illness has made me realize I'm not doing myself any favors by working around the clock.''

"Good. I'm glad to hear it. Now, what little bomb are you getting ready to drop on me?'' He winked.

Domini laughed. "I'd like to work a four-day week so I can have a longer weekend off.''

Carter sat back in the chair, touching his fingertips together. "Go on.''

"That's all, really. You see, while I was in Maui, I became friendly with a group of tourists and we did a lot of sailing together. I had no idea how exciting it could be. As it turns out, some of these people live near Tacoma and run a sailing school there. They've invited me to come down when I'm free. They've even offered to instruct me. Except during hurricanes, they sail just about every day of the year.''

"You didn't fall in love, did you?''

"Only with sailing.''

"More's the pity.'' He squinted at her. "What else is on your mind?''

"I know you've wanted me to do the Spokane tour but I don't think I'm ready for that much pressure yet.''

"I agree.''

"You do?''

"You'll always be my favorite Story Princess, Dom, but it occurred to me while you were in Bremerton that I can't expect it to last forever. Don't get me wrong. You created the role. It's yours for as long as you want it, but—"

"But being the tycoon that you are, you've got someone else in mind," she finished for him. Strangely enough, the idea didn't bother her at all. "Helen?"

"She's been training under you for three years."

"And she's younger."

"I've thought of calling her the Story Pixie, because she's pocket-size, and giving her more exposure."

"We could alternate the weekly shows!" Domini said enthusiastically. "She could go to Spokane!"

Carter looked pensive. "I'm postponing the tour for a while until you're ready, but Helen could take some of the load from you, both on television and at the recording end. I think a four-day week makes perfect sense, and it'll give Helen an opportunity to prove herself."

Domini winced as she recalled Jarod's words about Carter being a manipulator. Though she'd tried to set him straight, she didn't believe for one minute that Jarod had changed his opinion.

"Carter, I can't thank you enough," she finally replied with heartfelt gratitude.

"That works both ways, my dear. Your role as the Story Princess launched this company in a brand new direction. We have no competitors because there's only one Domini Loring."

"Thank you," she whispered in a tremulous voice.

He grinned. "I wish your father was still around so I could thank him for supporting your decision to work for me, despite his own disappointment. Have you ever regretted it?''

She shook her head. ''No, not at all. I've loved my work and I have enough opportunities to sing classical music away from the studio.''

''But not if you're sailing.''

''My work has always been indoors. This makes a wonderful change.'' Her face brightened as she spoke.

''You've just given me an idea. The Sailing Princess.''

''Oh, no,'' she chuckled, getting up from her chair. ''Can you imagine the state of that wig in the sea breezes?''

Carter roared with laughter as he accompanied her to the door. He threw his arm around her and planted a kiss on her forehead. ''Good luck, my dear. May you find what you're searching for. It will only be what you deserve.''

When Domini returned to her apartment at the end of the day, she felt a tremendous sense of relief. Carter had been even more understanding than she'd imagined, and she could make plans to run down to Tacoma for the weekend without any feelings of guilt.

She switched on the television while she ate a salad, but instead of watching the news, she found herself staring at the beautiful rose tree she'd placed on the coffee table. She couldn't stop thinking about those moments when Jarod had been loving and tender. It was like pressing compulsively on a sore tooth. The roses symbolized a time of supreme happiness, an ephemeral period of joy that had come to an end.

Her thoughts turned constantly to the children, as well, and the disastrous Christmas morning phone call that had left them in tears. Even worse was Jarod's polite, formal thank-you for all their gifts, delivered without the slightest hint of emotion in his voice. His manner was so remote, he might have been a stranger.

During her month in Hawaii, she'd started to write the boys a letter, then tore it up. She made a dozen attempts but couldn't possibly think of anything to say that would ease the ache in their hearts. Perhaps a clean break was best, but she knew they both suffered from the separation just as she did. She stared at the framed photograph they'd given her for Christmas. Jarod must have taken it when they were out sailing. Her only regret was that he wasn't in the picture with them.

The doorbell rang while she was in the kitchen putting the rest of the salad away. Supposing it to be her neighbor, she hurried across the living room to answer it, dressed in a faded flannel nightgown, her feet bare. With the chain still on, she opened the door, then sank weakly against it, clinging to the handle.

Jarod stood on the other side of the door, wearing a conservative dark suit and tie. She hadn't expected ever to see him again and stared up at him in shock. Even in the dim light he appeared pale. He looked leaner than usual, his features sharpened, as if by grief or rage.

"Jarod." She was too overcome by the brilliance of his eyes to think or move.

"May I come in?" The deep, rich voice that haunted her nights resonated through her body.

She tried to catch her breath. "I-I don't think—"

"We have to talk," he went on as if she'd never spoken. "Are you going to open the door or do I have to break it down? I'd do it without any compunction whatsoever."

The violence in him staggered her. She knew he meant it and actually felt faint. "Give me a moment to get dressed."

"Unfasten the chain, Domini." The threat in his voice had her shakily releasing the catch. Before she lowered her arm, he'd moved inside and shut the door behind him. Something about his quiet determination—even more than his aggression—alarmed her.

He turned to her and they faced each other at last, like old enemies. He was the first to speak. "All this time I thought you were in Spokane on tour," he said tightly. "I called the studio to find out when you'd be back, and your receptionist said you were on leave for an indeterminate period." His eyes narrowed. "Where have you been, Domini? Obviously not in Washington with a tan like that!"

She gazed at the floor, the blood pounding in her ears. He'd been trying to locate her. *Why?* "I took your advice and went on a long vacation." She finally dared to look at him. "Are the children all right?"

"That's debatable. Would it have been so difficult to drop them a line?"

She folded her arms protectively around her stomach. "Under the circumstances it seemed wiser not to write. Peter and Michael know they can always find me at the studio."

"How could they possibly do that when you haven't been there since you left Bremerton?"

"I decided to stay on in Maui until the doctor gave me a clean bill of health."

His hands clenched at his sides. "So that's where you've been. I hope you consulted a specialist."

"Yes. I did."

"And?"

"He said I'm fully recovered. Now, if that's everything I—"

"No, it's not!" He came closer, so close that she could breathe in his clean masculine scent. "Did you vacation alone?"

Domini couldn't believe he was asking her all these questions. They'd said goodbye a month ago. "What interest could that be to you?"

In a lightning move he cupped her chin in his hand and lifted her face. Despite herself, the touch of his fingers sent tiny waves of delight through her body. "Because I have to know if another man has held you in his arms and made love to you since you left Bremerton. Tell me."

"Jarod—" A rush of emotion forced her eyes closed and she clutched at the hand that gripped her chin to keep from falling.

"Jarod, what?" he demanded, grasping her by the upper arms. "Do you have any idea the hell I've been through wondering where you were, imagining you with someone else? I don't know about you, but I've had about all the sleepless nights I can take."

Dazed by his admission, she lifted luminescent green eyes to him, but his dark head blotted out the light and his mouth claimed hers. The unrestrained hunger of his kiss made her feel limp with desire. She was caught up in a voluptuous warmth that had her clinging to him, yielding to his demands. Moaning his name, she gave him kiss for kiss, intoxicated by the feel of his warm flesh beneath her hands as they slid inside his jacket.

"Domini—" He cried out as a shudder passed through his powerful body. "I want you and I *know* you want me," he whispered huskily against her throat. His caresses grew more passionate. His lips sought her eyes and flushed cheeks, but inevitably returned to her mouth. "Let me make love to you, Domini. I don't care what I told you earlier," he muttered against the heated skin of her neck. "You make me feel things that drive everything else out of my head."

When he would have picked her up in his arms, Domini found the strength to back away and put some distance between them. She grasped the back of a chair for support.

His words had the effect of dropping her from a great height. He'd never once mentioned *loving* her. What he talked about was *wanting* her—nothing more than a night's gratification.

He pulled off his tie and tossed it onto the couch. "What is it, Domini? Am I going too fast for you? You can't deny this was inevitable, not after what we started earlier." His eyes burned like blue flames, licking her with heat.

"I'm not denying anything," she finally said in a dull voice, feeling her heart die for the second time.

"I've been rearranging my schedule so we can have this coming weekend together. I have access to a cabin on the Peninsula, away from everyone else—no phones, no one to bother us."

She struggled to find the right words. Everything in her cried out to say yes. Three days and nights with Jarod tempted her almost beyond endurance. But what about the rest of her life? What about the thousands of days and nights she'd lie alone in her bed when he didn't want her anymore? She wanted the right to share his whole life, not just a few stolen moments of ecstasy. She wanted his babies. His heart and soul.

"I can't." Her answer came out in a muffled voice.

"Give me one good reason why not. Can you deny that you want this as much as I do?"

"I have another commitment for this weekend, Jarod. I can't cancel it now."

His head reared back and she could tell he was barely holding on to his control. "All right, then we'll plan to go away the following weekend."

"That isn't possible right now. I've been away from the studio almost three months."

"Domini..." he murmured, drawing her toward him, wrapping her in his arms. "I've been doing a lot of thinking about us," he whispered into her hair. "A weekend with you isn't really what I want at all. It isn't enough," he said huskily. He began to cover her eyes, her lips, her throat with hot, passionate kisses. Taking her face in his hands, he said, "Stay with me tonight. I know a little place out of town we can have to ourselves. If we can't go away together, let's at least take advantage of the times when I come into Seattle."

His face had an eager, tremulous look of joy as he stared down at her, but something was wrong and she couldn't share his excitement. Had she misunderstood, or was he expecting to have an affair with her?

"What about the children?"

"What about them?" he asked in a voice thick with emotion. "Mrs. Maughan is there to watch out for them whenever I'm away—you know that. What you and I share will remain private. I'll come to Seattle more often."

He *was* asking her to have an affair with him! She hadn't thought he could hurt her anymore, but she was wrong.

"You've gone so quiet. What is it?" He pulled far enough away to look down at her. "If you'd rather stay here, it's fine with me. I don't care where we sleep as long as it's together."

"You're an exciting man, Jarod. And I can't deny that I'm... attracted to you. I couldn't hide it if I wanted to, but I'm not interested in casual affairs."

His jaw hardened. "Have I ever implied that I thought you were?"

Her delicate brow furrowed. "I'm not sure. When you came to my office that first time, you accused me of saying or doing anything for publicity's sake. You didn't bother to conceal your low opinion of me."

"That was before I got to know you," he thundered.

"And now that you think you know me, you're asking me to sleep with you," she stated in an even voice.

"You're distorting my words," he said through gritted teeth. "I know the real Domini Loring and I want her in my bed and in my life."

Domini fought to hold back the angry tears. "But only in the dark and only away from your home—and your family."

"You're the Story Princess, for heaven's sake! You have an image to protect."

"And a discreet affair with you wouldn't endanger my reputation," she said hotly.

He looked furious. "Who said anything about an affair? I've just told you I want you to be part of my life. We'll be discreet so that when we're around the boys, they'll never know."

"Someone always finds out, Jarod. What if I got pregnant?"

His eyes blazed with a new light. "Then I'd take care of you and the baby forever. Can you doubt it?" His voice was hoarse. "Domini—I need you."

She turned aside. "And what about my needs?"

His hands came around her from behind, and he pulled her close. "Don't you know I'd do everything in my power to fulfill them? Do you have any idea how much I ache to love you?" His mouth against the tender skin of her neck acted like a drug, leaving her lethargic with desire. Weakening her resistance...

She lowered her head, giving him easier access. "I'll have to think about it," she whispered, so close to surrendering that she was really frightened.

"What is there to think about?" he groaned and turned her toward him. But when he bent to kiss her, she moved away.

"Too many things. The affair will end one day. I have to think about that—and the fact that I've never been with a man before. For me, it would be a tremendous step to take."

He caught her hands between his and kissed the palms with a sweet, seductive tenderness. "Do you mean to tell me you've never made love before?" he asked incredulously.

She pulled out of his grasp. "No. You see, Jarod, there's quite a lot you don't know about me. I need some time."

Jarod rubbed his hand against his chest. One dark brow slanted in puzzlement. "Have you ever been in love, Domini?"

"I thought I was, once."

"Carter?"

She looked at him, her eyes clear and steady. "Roberto Verrini."

He blinked. "The tenor?"

She nodded. "He singled me out at the opera auditions in Rome, called me his American Beauty rose. I fell madly in love until I found out he called Gerda his German edelweiss and Anita his Mexican poppy."

Jarod threw back his head and laughed. The sound of his delight brought a half smile to her lips as he once more gathered her into his arms. He buried his face in her neck, still chuckling, then tugged gently on her earlobe with his teeth. "Oh, Domini..." he groaned. "I know why I'm so crazy about you. I never know what you're going to say next. How long are you going to keep me waiting for my answer?" There was no mirth in his voice now.

She lay against his shoulder, luxuriating in his warmth and strength, but in her heart she already knew the answer. She loved Jarod, but she would never settle for less than marriage. She supposed he might love her a little—but not enough for a lifetime commitment. Perhaps he was still emotionally bound to his wife. Whatever the reason, having an affair with him would only hurt her, might even destroy her. And she'd end up alone.

Slowly she moved out of his arms and put some distance between them. "I'll give it to you now. To paraphrase your words the night before I left Bremerton, I want to come to you, but if I do, I might live to regret it. For reasons I won't go into, the answer has to be no."

His stillness told her more than all his arguments, all his protestations. "I won't ask again," he vowed.

"I know."

She thought he was going to say something else. His blue eyes shot her a challenge that flickered, then died. In an instant, he was gone.

FEBRUARY PASSED as the bleakest month Domini had ever known. She wondered if she would ever recover from the pain of losing Jarod. Only with the deaths of her parents had she experienced anything similar. Once again, she buried herself in work, to keep from thinking about Jarod twenty-four hours a day. If she didn't fall into bed until she was exhausted, she'd manage to get some sleep. Her one pleasure was sailing on the weekends.

Domini was scheduled to sing with the oratorio society at the opera house the last night of the month. Rehearsals of *The Messiah*, following her demanding workdays, kept her too busy to dwell on her unhappiness.

The night of the performance she dressed in a full-length white crepe gown and wore a rope of pearls around her neck. Her hair had grown even longer in the past month, hiding the pearl earrings that had been Jarod's Christmas gift—something she'd treasure all her life.

On the whole, she felt she sang well, particularly the passage that had been her father's favorite, "He Shall Feed His Sheep." The cast and orchestra performed to a packed house. Afterward, Domini and the other singers stood backstage amid the clutter and chaos, accepting the congratulations of well-wishers. People were pressing in on them from all sides. She was on the verge of leaving when she felt a tug on her dress. She glanced down and caught sight of a shiny blond head. The child was clutching her dress with tight, desperate fingers.

"Michael?" Her cry of joy caused several heads to turn as she swept him up in her arms. "I can't believe it!"

"I told Mrs. Maughan you'd be happy to see me." He smiled the sweet smile she remembered and hugged her around the neck until he almost strangled her.

"Where is she? Where's Peter?"

He loosened his hold and looked around the crowd from his perch in his arms. "Over there." He pointed in the direction of one of the side stairs. On an impulse, she kissed him. In the excitement of seeing Michael, Domini's heart ran away with her. "Is your father here, too?" she asked as she struggled through the crowd, holding Michael as if he belonged to her.

"No. Daddy's away on a long trip to Los Angeles. We couldn't go because we had school, but he said he'd take us with him next time."

"I see," she whispered, depressed in a strange new way. Had he traveled for business or pleasure? More important, had he taken a woman with him? The idea of anyone else receiving his love drove her out of her mind, but she couldn't ask the children.

"There she is," she heard Peter cry. He was weaving through the crowd, he'd almost reached her. Domini set Michael down and bent to kiss his brother on the cheek, hugging him hard. Both boys were wearing the sweaters she'd made them.

"Peter," she said tearfully as she felt his arms around her. "I've missed you more than you'll ever know."

"I feel the same," he said, staring up at her with eyes too wise for his years. "Daddy wouldn't let me call you, but we saw you at the concert, so he can't get mad about that," he declared, grabbing her hand.

"Miss Loring...Domini," the housekeeper called out, having finally squeezed through to reach them. Her arrival prevented Domini from responding to Peter's painful statement. She gave the older woman an emotional hug, then offered a hand to each of the boys. They gripped hers tightly.

"The children and I decided we couldn't miss this when we found out you were one of the leads," Mrs. Maughan explained. "*The Messiah* will always remind us of the time you were in Bremerton."

"You sang pretty, Domini, but I like 'The Gingerbread Man' better," Michael inserted. Domini and Mrs. Maughan exchanged knowing glances and started to smile. It felt so right, the four of them laughing together. Domini couldn't believe they weren't back in Bremerton, almost like a family.

"I have a wonderful idea. How would the three of you like to come to my house? We can buy some Chinese food on the way home and have a party. I'm always starving after a performance. What do you say?"

Perhaps it was unfair to spring this on Mrs. Maughan, but Domini couldn't help herself. She'd missed the children so much, and she couldn't see how one night with them could hurt. Jarod wasn't there to disapprove, but if he had been, she'd have willingly stood up to him. She loved the boys, and she knew they craved time with her as she did with them.

"Could we, Mrs. Maughan?" they asked excitedly.

Domini decided to go all the way. "If you have something you want to do in Seattle, why don't you let the boys spend the night with me, Mrs. Maughan? That way we can stay up as late as we want and sleep in tomorrow. I've got a sofa bed in the living room that will sleep them both."

The boys' eyes fastened on her as if she were some celestial being. They were too awed by her proposal to talk.

The housekeeper smiled at Domini. "If you're sure it won't be too much trouble, I think it's a splendid idea. They've missed you," she added in a lower voice. "My sister lives in the city and I can spend the night with her. She's old and it's hard on her to have the children around."

"Why don't you let me keep the boys for the whole weekend, then, unless that's not convenient. I don't have to work until Monday."

Mrs. Maughan appeared pleased at the prospect. "I'll need your address so I can pick them up Sunday at noon. We'll have to get back to Bremerton in good time, because they have school the next day."

The crowd had thinned considerably by the time Domini had given Mrs. Maughan directions and they'd said their goodbyes. Still, Michael and Peter clung to her and she didn't want any of it to stop. Being with them was a joy in itself, but it was also a link to Jarod. Certain of their comments and mannerisms brought Jarod so forcefully to mind, Domini could hardly bear it.

She ushered them out of the opera house to her car, and they stopped to pick up some Chinese food on the route to her place. She had a hard time fitting in questions about Jarod because they fought so hard to fill her in on every detail of their lives since she'd left them. Domini treasured each word.

Long after they'd eaten and settled down for bed, the three of them were still talking nonstop. These stolen hours might have to last her a lifetime. The revelation that Jarod had been in a bad mood since Christmas made her wonder if he missed her, until Peter suddenly blurted out, "Why did Daddy kiss you if he dislikes you so much?"

He couldn't have wounded her more if he'd plunged a dagger in her heart. "I can't answer that, Peter. Grown-ups act strangely at times and we don't always know why."

"I hate him."

Domini crouched beside him and gently patted his arm. "Don't say that, darling. He loves you very, very much."

"No, he doesn't. He's meaner than my principal. I'd rather live with you, but I know I can't. When I grow up I'm going to go far away from him. So's Michael." He heaved a shuddery sigh that went right through her. It sounded as if Jarod's home was in turmoil, which only compounded her pain. "Domini, can we go to the Seattle Aquarium tomorrow?" Peter's unexpected request reminded her to cancel her weekend sailing date.

"I think that's a wonderful idea. I haven't been there since my dad took me years ago. Now, let's get some sleep so we can keep up with Michael tomorrow." Michael had finally passed out from sheer exhaustion.

"You're nice," Peter said as his eyelids dropped. "Domini—I love you."

She swallowed hard. "I love you, too, Peter." One salty tear trickled down her cheek and onto his as she leaned over to kiss him good-night.

Domini carried a new weight in her heart when she went to work the following week. Saying goodbye to the children was one of the hardest things she'd ever had to do. She couldn't promise to see them again, and they didn't ask.

The house was so empty without their vivacious little spirits, she dreaded coming home to it each night. Her life felt shallow and unfulfilled since Jarod had gone. Though she liked her work, she felt as if she were standing on the periphery of her world, looking in on it, but never part of it—never experiencing the real stuff of life.

CHAPTER TEN

"MISS LORING? This is Mrs. Maughan."

"Yes, Mrs. Maughan? Is something wrong?" Domini had barely walked in the door from work when the phone rang. She hadn't even taken off her coat. She gripped the receiver tightly. The housekeeper wouldn't be calling if something weren't wrong with Jarod or the boys.

"Before I tell you why I'm calling, let me assure you that everyone's fine, so you can take the worry out of your voice."

"Thank heavens." Domini sighed her heartfelt relief. "You've all been on my mind since you left Sunday morning."

"Yes, well, you should be at my end. It's Domini this and Domini that. Which brings me to the reason for my call. My daughter's twins have bad colds and ear infections, and she's at her wit's end because she's lost so much sleep. She insists she'll be all right but I think she needs me. There's only one problem. I haven't been in this particular situation before, and with Dr. Wolfe away—"

"You want me to come and stay with the boys?" Domini anticipated the housekeeper's request, already mentally working out what she'd have to do to manage it.

"If you could! They love you, and above all, they trust you. I wouldn't feel good about leaving them with anyone else, even though some of their friends' parents would probably take them if I asked. They have an aunt on their mother's side who lives in Coeur d'Alene, Idaho, but they don't feel a bit close to her. I don't think Dr. Wolfe would want me to contact her. As a last resort, I can call Dr. Wolfe but—"

"No," Domini interrupted, her heart pounding. "That's not necessary. I finally have a way to repay my debt to you for your wonderful nursing care when I was so ill." She moistened her lips. "When is Jarod expected home?"

"Not for three weeks. He's only been gone one so far. There's a medical convention in L.A. He decided to combine that with a vacation—his first in years. He's meeting some friends there. He's been going nonstop since his wife died, and I think he needs the time away. That's why I'm reluctant to call him."

"Don't! You should be with your daughter right now. Nothing else matters, and there's no place I'd rather be than with the children."

"But can you take the time off from your work?"

"It doesn't matter if I can or not. I will. I'll come tonight. It might be close to midnight but I'll make it."

"There's only one problem. I don't know how long I'll be away."

"I'll be there for the children until you can come back. Please don't worry about it. I know what it's like when loved ones are sick."

"I knew I could count on you. Then I'll see you tonight. The outside lights will be on. Be careful on the highway."

"I will. Now call your daughter and tell her everything's been taken care of. She'll be relieved just to know that."

"You're an angel, Miss Loring—Domini. I'll never forget this."

Domini hung up the phone and hugged her arms to her chest in excitement. Suddenly, nothing was as important as being with the children.

She kept trying to reach Carter while she packed, but to no avail. In the end, she left a message on his answering machine, explaining that she'd been summoned away on an emergency and would call him when she could. With that off her mind, she asked her neighbor to look in on her place, then loaded the car.

By nine-thirty, she was on her way to Seattle to get the ferry. Many a night Jarod had driven this same road, and somehow the thought made her feel closer to him. Did he ever think about her during the long stretches of solitude?

As she left the bridge it occurred to her that Jarod would be calling the boys from time to time. She would have to make sure she kept the answering machine on when they were at school. If he did find out she was taking care of his children, she'd rely on Mrs. Maughan to explain.

Domini refused to think about the day she'd have to leave the children again. That day would come soon enough.

True to her prediction, it was twelve-thirty by the time she pulled into the driveway. Even before she'd turned off the headlights, the children dashed out of the house and converged on her. Their shrieks of delight were carried away in the wind that blew over the Sound.

Without waiting to be told, they lugged her cases into the house, insisting that she sleep with them in the loft. Peter took one look at her mandolin and begged her to teach him how to play.

"Maybe tomorrow, but right now it's time for you two to get into bed. Mrs. Maughan needs to leave and she has to give me instructions before she goes."

She kissed them good-night and tucked them in their bunk beds, then hurried down to the kitchen to talk to the housekeeper.

"Mrs. Maughan?" Domini found her putting her suitcase by the front door. "Is someone coming for you or are you taking a taxi to your daughter's?"

"My son-in-law will be over in just a little while. I've left my daughter's phone number on the pad, as well as the number where Dr. Wolfe can be reached in case of an emergency. He phones every night to talk to the boys, except that he didn't call them tonight for some reason. Anyway, I think that's everything. I put the car keys by the pad so you can drive the children to school and run errands."

Domini rubbed her hands along her hips. "I think you ought to know that Jarod wouldn't like it if he knew I was here taking care of his children."

The older woman smiled. "I've had complete charge of those boys for almost five years. Finding someone to replace me in an emergency is my decision, and I happen to believe you're the right person. The children's welfare will always come first with me. I love them, and I happen to know you love them, too. That's all there is to it! He's never questioned my judgment. He wouldn't dare."

As Mrs. Maughan continued to answer Domini's questions about the running of the house and the children's routine, they heard a car pull into the driveway.

"That will be my son-in-law. Goodbye for now, Domini. One day I hope you'll know just how grateful I am."

"It's a small enough return, considering everything you did for me before Christmas. We're even." Domini gave her a hug and opened the door to assist her. Then she gasped. The man coming up the walk, carrying a suitcase and shoulder bag, was Jarod. Domini felt the blood drain out of her face as he approached.

The porch light revealed lines of fatigue around his eyes and mouth. Domini thought he'd lost a little weight and he was unshaved—yet he looked more attractive to her at this moment than ever before.

He went completely still when he saw the two of them standing at the entrance. His eyes darted first to Domini, then Mrs. Maughan. Domini wanted to fade into the woodwork.

"Well, well." Mrs. Maughan broke the silence. "Running away didn't solve a thing, did it?"

Domini had never heard Mrs. Maughan treat Jarod with anything but the highest respect, and she was shocked to hear the mockery in the older woman's voice.

Jarod slowly lowered his bags to the ground and placed his hands on his hips. "So, now that all the players are assembled, would someone mind telling me what is going on in my own home? Or would that be too much to ask?"

Mrs. Maughan's chin lifted defiantly. "It wouldn't be if you weren't so blind."

"You sound just like you used to when one of us residents got your back up over something we did wrong. Out with it, Mrs. Maughan."

"For such a wonderful doctor, you're positively obtuse when it comes to your personal life."

Jarod's mouth tightened. "So you thought you'd shed a little light on the situation, is that right?"

"Jarod—" Domini felt compelled to intervene at this point. "The twins are sick and Mrs. Maughan needed someone to watch out for the boys so she could go and be with her daughter. Her son-in-law will be here any moment."

His eyes met hers for the first time. "Considering that Pam and Dennis and the twins are vacationing in Arizona this month, she might have rather a long wait."

Shaking her head in complete confusion, Domini looked at Mrs. Maughan for an explanation. She could hear the patter of feet running down the hall and Michael's shout of joy when he discovered their father was home. Peter was more subdued.

"Dad? What are you doing home so soon?"

Jarod leaned over and scooped Michael into his arms, tousling Peter's hair at the same time. "I didn't have a good time because I missed you guys too much, so I came back. I brought some presents for you. Why don't you take my bags into the living room and find them while I talk to Mrs. Maughan and Domini for a minute."

Michael's cry of delight shook the house as he and Peter disappeared down the hall.

"Before you start jumping to conclusions, Jarod Wolfe, remember that I asked Miss Loring to come here and stay with the children," Mrs. Maughan asserted in a superior tone of voice that would have shriveled a lesser person. "And if I chose to lie about the reason, then that's my affair and no one else's."

The housekeeper's admission that she'd called her on false pretenses made Domini's thoughts reel. "But I don't understand," she murmured, looking from Mrs. Maughan to Jarod. His shuttered expression gave nothing away.

"Domini, would you mind waiting for me inside? I'd like to talk to Mrs. Maughan in private."

"Yes, of course." Domini glanced at Mrs. Maughan before turning away, puzzled by the strange glint in the older woman's eyes; she seemed almost . . . pleased by the whole situation.

"Come and play doctor with me," Michael urged the minute she walked into the living room. He held up a toy doctor's kit Jarod had brought him.

"You should both be in bed," she told them, watching Peter out of the corner of her eye. A box containing a model sailboat that had to be assembled lay unopened on the table.

"Domini, could I play with your mandolin for a little while?" Peter asked quietly. She didn't have the heart to refuse him.

"Maybe for a few minutes, but then you'll have to go to bed."

"Thanks." He dashed upstairs to the loft where she'd left it, while Michael yanked on her arm and begged her to lie on the floor.

"Pretend you've been in a motorcycle accident."

"Am I very sick?" It was difficult if not impossible to get into the spirit of Michael's game when she was desperate to know what Jarod and Mrs. Maughan were discussing.

"You're almost dead," Michael muttered seriously as he put the stethoscope around his neck and pulled on a pair of rubber gloves.

Domini smoothed her navy sweatshirt over her jeans then arranged herself on the floor. She moaned aloud several times and pressed the back of her hand to her forehead.

He pulled off one of her tennis shoes and tapped the bottom of her foot to test her reflexes, then tapped her knees. "Your leg is broken. I'll have to put on a cast." He wrapped an elastic bandage around her calf with amazing dexterity.

"You're going to have to have a shot for the pain." He took an enormous plastic syringe from the satchel and poked her arm in several spots. "You have a bump on your forehead. Here's an ice pack." He plopped it on her face. "Now I have to listen to your heart."

"I think this is where I ought to take over."

"Daddy!" Michael scrambled to his feet and threw himself into his father's arms.

Domini's heart literally skipped a beat, and she felt as ill as she'd pretended to be moments earlier. The ice pack covered one eye. She wished it covered the other, too, because she was terrified to look at Jarod for fear of what she'd see.

"It's time for you and Peter to get to bed. Run along and I'll be up to tuck you in after I've talked to Domini."

Michael obediently said good-night to both of them and thanked his father for his present before hurrying out of the living room. She and Jarod were finally alone.

She expected him to ask her to leave as soon as possible. Slowly she turned her head and gazed at him. He'd removed his tie and unbuttoned his collar. She could see the strong column of throat where a pulse throbbed. Her own pulse could match his, beat for beat. "I know you never wanted to see me again, but please don't make a scene while the boys are still up. Now that you're back, I'll go."

"I have no intention of upsetting the children." Instead, he crouched next to her and pushed her gently back to the floor. "I wonder if your heart gives you away when you're caught off guard? I think I'll find out."

She gasped as he placed the metal part of the stethoscope over her left breast and listened. His eyes darkened. "It's beating out of rhythm, which means your adrenal glands are working overtime." He withdrew the instrument, but the shocking touch of his fingers against her body stayed with her, immobilizing her. "I want an explanation from you, but not until the children are in bed."

"Where's Mrs. Maughan?"

"In her room. I canceled the taxi she called."

"I-I see." Domini could hardly get the words out.

"I doubt it." After a sustained pause he said, "Michael did a nice job of wrapping that leg. I'll make a doctor of him yet."

Unable to tolerate any more, Domini jumped to her feet. She was intensely aware of Jarod's eyes on her. The sensuality of his gaze both disturbed and excited her. Her clothes were perfectly adequate, yet she had the feeling he could see through them.

"Whatever Mrs. Maughan's reasons for what she did, it's probably my fault that she called me. You see, the boys happened to see me when they went to *The Messiah* with her. They came backstage and one thing led to another and I invited them to spend the weekend with me. We had such a lovely time, it was difficult to say goodbye. Peter didn't want to go."

"Peter loves you," Jarod stated unequivocally. "He's been upset since the day he entered that contest and won! Mrs. Maughan knew the only way you'd ever set foot inside this house was to get you here on one pretext or another so he'd calm down. What astounds me is that you came!" His voice shook.

Domini gazed at him searchingly. "Why do you say that? I love your children as much as if they were my own. I know you don't believe that, but it's true. I was so thrilled to be asked to look after them, I left Seattle without even talking to Carter."

Her declaration caused his eyes to burn a feverish blue. "Don't you think I want to believe you?" he grated.

She shook her head in bewilderment. "What holds you back, Jarod? I've never understood."

In an instant, all expression was wiped from his face. "Amanda said she loved me and Peter, but there was always a story to investigate, another assignment to go out on. I came to realize almost from the day we got married that she was a career woman in the most literal sense of the word.

"No matter what plans we made as a family, no matter what holiday or special occasion, her work came first. She missed out on the important events in Peter's life because of her job. We fought day and night as a result.

"I rearranged my schedule as much as I could so we could try to find a little more time to be together. But it was a mistake—it only made matters worse. She spent any time I managed to free up not with us but at the station, or socializing with her single friends. Then we had another baby, which she considered an accident, a mistake. She refused to take care of Michael or learn how to be a mother. The miracle is that we found a night she was home long enough to get pregnant!"

Domini sank down on the couch because her legs would no longer support her. Jarod paced back and forth, rubbing his neck as he continued to reveal the source of his bitterness.

"One day I woke up and realized I didn't love her anymore. Whatever I'd felt for her had died. Perhaps that's why I felt partly responsible for what went wrong between us.

"When we met she was a young reporter doing a story about the activities on the Sound for a documentary on its history. She showed up on the pier one day and asked a lot of questions. I was attracted, but also vulnerable because my brother, Adam, had recently died. She brought diversion into my life when I needed it most.

"I was still in medical school and hesitant to marry, but she pushed for it. Like a fool I went along with it because suddenly the idea of a stable home life and a family sounded appealing. She didn't tell me until after the ceremony that she didn't want children for a long time. We argued over it continually, but despite that, Peter came along."

So many thoughts converged in Domini's head, she was almost dizzy. All this time she'd thought he couldn't love anyone else.... Everything started to fall into place—she finally understood his distrust of her, his hostility toward her job, with its high public profile. It all made a horrible kind of sense. But Jarod was too absorbed in his explanation to notice her reaction.

"We had a fight on the day she died. I begged her to go back to work *part*-time because Michael was only four months old. She wouldn't compromise and made it clear that being a mother wasn't for her.

"I threatened her with divorce if she continued to go off every day—sometimes for a week at a time—leaving the welfare of the children to me and the latest baby-sitter. Peter needed her desperately and was devastated by her absences. I felt it would be better if she and I went our separate ways. I couldn't bear for the children to hear us quarreling."

The picture he painted made Domini want to weep. She couldn't imagine putting anything or anyone before Jarod! No wonder she, Domini, had always been suspect in his eyes. If only she'd known the truth about Amanda from the beginning, so much misunderstanding could have been avoided. Her heart ached for him and the misery of his broken marriage. It explained Peter's needs as nothing else could have done. And all Michael wanted was to be loved!

"God may not forgive me for this but after the funeral I felt nothing. No real sorrow. No regret," he confessed. "I just made up my mind to be the best single parent I could be. Mrs. Maughan had lost her husband some time earlier and I asked her to come and work for me. I'd always admired her warmth and character. To my everlasting gratitude, she accepted my offer. Peter took to her at once, and she's been with us ever since.

"We managed to get on well enough. Until a few months ago, I thought our family had healed." His pained eyes met hers in a speaking glance. "The results of the children winning that contest made one thing crystal clear. I would never be able to meet some of Peter's needs, because he'd been starving for a mother's love, something he never knew with Amanda. It was love at first sight when you took the boys around the studio. It's very simple, really—you gave of yourself, you were there for them. And as a result, you won my children's eternal devotion."

His words thrilled her but she wanted to hear that *he* couldn't live without her.

He stopped pacing. "The night we went to dinner and you told me we couldn't visit you in Seattle because you'd be on tour convinced me that it was Amanda all over again—but so much worse because the children worshiped the ground you walked on. I didn't know how I could tell Peter that you weren't available, that you might never be. I didn't want that whole syndrome of waiting and aching to start again. He'd spent too many years hoping for something that would never happen and I wanted to spare him."

"If only I'd known." Domini shook her head.

"You'd still have gone on tour!" he insisted, his eyes dark with defeat.

"That's true, but I would have phoned him before I left Seattle and made definite plans so we'd both have something to look forward to."

"Both?" he asked warily.

"I had the time of my life with your children. I missed them dreadfully, and I would have accepted your invitation in an instant if the tour hadn't already been planned. Why do you think I came to Bremerton? As soon as Carter gave me time off, I had Bill drive me here, even though I felt wretched."

He didn't say anything for a minute. "You should have seen their eyes when they heard you were in town."

The emotion in his voice told her so much. "I didn't know what to think," he went on. "Your coming to Bremerton convinced the children that they were of vital importance in your life, and I couldn't talk them out of it. Your power over them terrified me."

"But don't you see," she said softly, "they were... *are* of vital importance, Jarod. They always will be because I love them. I can't explain why. I didn't give birth to them, but I can't imagine loving a child of my own body more."

His jaw clenched. "I know. That kind of love isn't something you can fake for very long. When I walked in on you a few minutes ago and saw you lying there for no other purpose than to please Michael, something snapped inside me.

"I can see I've been wrong to keep the children from you. Peter chose sides a long time ago. Domini—" An incredible look of pleading entered his eyes and voice. "I lived with Amanda long enough to know that I can have no influence over you where your career is concerned, but I'm begging you to let the children be a part of your life. They need you."

Domini could barely restrain her tears. As much as she loved the children, she couldn't be around them and not have Jarod's love too. He was asking the impossible.

"Much as I adore them, I don't think it's a good idea. The separations just get more painful."

"You're right, of course." He raked both hands through his hair in a frantic gesture. "I had no right to ask that of you. I'm sorry."

Afraid she'd break down in front of him, she muttered something about going upstairs to pack and fled from the living room.

"Domini?" he cried as she disappeared up the staircase toward his room. He dashed after her and caught her by the shoulders just inside the bedroom door.

"Domini—" He pulled her against his chest from behind. "Don't go. Don't leave me. I'm so in love with you I can't think straight."

His lips covered every inch of skin till he found her mouth. He twisted her in his arms, urging her closer, closer, until they moved and breathed as one flesh. "You're the most beautiful, exciting, heavenly thing to ever come into my life. You've got to marry me, Domini," he whispered huskily. "Maybe one day you'll be able to return my love. All I'm begging for is a chance."

Domini leaned far enough away to look up at him. "Mrs. Maughan was right. You're as blind as the proverbial bat, Jarod. She knew I was so much in love with you that I . . . Well, let me show you." Her hands reached to caress the sides of his face.

She saw an explosion of tiny blue lights in his eyes and then his mouth was on hers. An eternity seemed to pass as they stood twined together, one silhouette against the moonlight spilling through the window.

"Are you going to sing at our wedding?" Michael piped up, staring unabashedly at the two of them.

Jarod managed to recover first. Domini heard him groan, then felt his shoulders shake before he broke into full-bodied laughter. He enfolded Domini in his arms to allow her time to pull herself together.

"I think this is one wedding where her singing won't be required, Michael." He kissed her full on the mouth, taking his time about it as Peter turned on the bedroom light, still holding her mandolin. Domini gazed in wonder at the love shining out of Jarod's eyes.

"Our Story Princess is going to be the bride. In white, I think," he muttered sensuously, "and just as soon as possible or this groom refuses to be held accountable for the consequences."

"What's consequences?" Michael wanted to know.

"Come back to bed, children," Mrs. Maughan ordered, appearing in the bedroom in her robe and nightgown. "Leave your poor parents to make their plans in peace. What your father was referring to is a little matter concerning hormones."

Jarod's bark of laughter filled the bedroom. "Hormones? Mrs. Maughan, you're priceless. Little did you know that your devious plot to get Domini back in this house was unnecessary." He hugged Domini tightly against him. "As soon as I'd left, I realized that all I really cared about was right here, and I vowed that the minute my meetings were over, I'd be back, begging Domini to marry me. Thanks to you, Mrs. Maughan, I didn't have to leave my own home to do it!"

Peter rubbed his tired eyes with his free hand. "It's about time, Dad. I had plans to run away to Domini's place so you'd have to come and get me. I guess you found out you were wrong about her, after all." The first real smile anyone had seen in months lighted his face.

"Yeah." Michael's little round chin went up. "You said she probably didn't like children and that she was an entirely different p-pro-a-si-shun when she went home."

Domini couldn't resist kissing Jarod's cheek. She'd never seen him blush before. "I'm surprised Peter didn't put *that* in the letter," she whispered.

He nuzzled her ear. "I think I'd better keep my mouth permanently shut around the boys from now on," he whispered back. "Maybe we'll just stay in the bedroom and make love for the rest of our lives. That way I'll stay out of trouble."

The children seemed to sense that their presence wasn't needed or acknowledged and left at Mrs. Maughan's urgings.

"Do you promise?" Domini gave him a seductive smile. "I want to feel our baby growing inside me. Peter and Michael have made me so hungry for the things I've been missing."

He inhaled deeply. "You don't know what hunger is, but you're going to find out. I swear I never saw anything so beautiful in my life as you standing there on the pavement that day. I felt as if you'd bewitched me. My children never stood a chance."

Domini kissed every part of his face and lingered on his mouth. "Since we're confessing things, I have to tell you that you weren't anything like I'd imagined, either. I pictured you as a financially destitute older man, completely irrational with grief."

He kissed her long and hard. "Instead you were confronted with a stranger who was completely irrational with desire. And maybe just plain irrational," he admitted ruefully.

"Actually—" Domini traced his mouth with her finger "—I was so crazy about you that I overlooked the bitterness to discover the wonderful man beneath.

You're the man I've been searching for all my life, make no mistake about it, Dr. Wolfe. I love you." Her voice trembled with longing.

A low sound of contentment eased out of him, but then he sobered. "Domini—I want you to know that much as I would like the Story Princess all to myself—forever—I wouldn't dream of asking you to give up your career to marry me. What I'm hoping is that we can work out a way for all of us to be happy and fulfilled."

Domini loved him for saying that, because she knew how long he'd struggled to be able to trust again. "I want that, too. So much, that I talked to Carter after I returned from Hawaii. I've been working a four-day-week for the past little while."

"I had no idea!" he cried out incredulously.

"And there's something else. He's training Helen to take on part of my job. How do you feel about the Story Pixie invading our living room every other week?"

"I love it," he whispered. "Forgive me if I'm still in shock."

She nestled closer. "I told Carter that I need time for myself. I'm sure anything you and I decide about my career will be fine with him." She took a deep breath. "You come first, Jarod."

"Domini, there's so much I want to show you, tell you, share with you. Do you think you could ever bring yourself to set foot on a boat again?" He placed a tender kiss on her neck. "I've had so many dreams and plans that I never expected to materialize."

She lifted shimmering green eyes to him, clasping his dear face between her hands. "Never forget that I have magic powers. *Anything* is possible, my love."

But Jarod had magic of his own, and he cast his own spell with his lips and hands . . . with his love. All the while, a certain someone in another part of the house made mental preparations to move closer to her daughter. She smiled secretly—thinking that a new fairy tale had just begun—but not without the help of a little sorcery from her.

H·I·S·T·O·R·I·C·A·L
Christmas
S·T·O·R·I·E·S 1·9·9·0

Once again Harlequin, the experts in romance, bring you the magic of Christmas —as celebrated in America's past.

These enchanting love stories celebrate Christmas made extra-special by the wonder of people in love....

Nora Roberts	**In From the Cold**
Patricia Potter	**Miracle of the Heart**
Ruth Langan	**Christmas at Bitter Creek**

Look for this Christmas collection now wherever Harlequin® books are sold.

"Makes a great stocking stuffer."

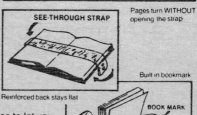

PASSPORT TO ROMANCE VACATION SWEEPSTAKES

OFFICIAL RULES

SWEEPSTAKES RULES AND REGULATIONS. NO PURCHASE NECESSARY.
HOW TO ENTER:

1. To enter, complete this official entry form and return with your invoice in the envelope provided, or print your name, address, telephone number and age on a plain piece of paper and mail to: Passport to Romance, P.O. Box #1397, Buffalo, N.Y. 14269-1397 No mechanically reproduced entries accepted.
2. All entries must be received by the Contest Closing Date, midnight, December 31, 1990 to be eligible.
3. Prizes: There will be ten (10) Grand Prizes awarded, each consisting of a choice of a trip for two people to: i) London, England (approximate retail value $5,050 U.S.); ii) England, Wales and Scotland (approximate retail value $6,400 U.S.); iii) Caribbean Cruise (approximate retail value $7,300 U.S.); iv) Hawaii (approximate retail value $ 9,550 U.S.); v) Greek Island Cruise in the Mediterranean (approximate retail value $12,250 U.S.); vi) France (approximate retail value $7,300 U.S.).
4. Any winner may choose to receive any trip or a cash alternative prize of $5,000.00 U.S. in lieu of the trip.
5. Odds of winning depend on number of entries received.
6. A random draw will be made by Nielsen Promotion Services, an independent judging organization on January 29, 1991, in Buffalo, N.Y., at 11:30 a.m. from all eligible entries received on or before the Contest Closing Date. Any Canadian entrants who are selected must correctly answer a time-limited, mathematical skill-testing question in order to win. Quebec residents may submit any litigation respecting the conduct and awarding of a prize in this contest to the Régie des loteries et courses du Quebec.
7. Full contest rules may be obtained by sending a stamped, self-addressed envelope to: "Passport to Romance Rules Request", P.O. Box 9998, Saint John, New Brunswick, E2L 4N4.
8. Payment of taxes other than air and hotel taxes is the sole responsibility of the winner.
9. Void where prohibited by law.

PASSPORT TO ROMANCE VACATION SWEEPSTAKES

OFFICIAL RULES

SWEEPSTAKES RULES AND REGULATIONS. NO PURCHASE NECESSARY.
HOW TO ENTER:

1. To enter, complete this official entry form and return with your invoice in the envelope provided, or print your name, address, telephone number and age on a plain piece of paper and mail to: Passport to Romance, P.O. Box #1397, Buffalo, N.Y. 14269-1397 No mechanically reproduced entries accepted.
2. All entries must be received by the Contest Closing Date, midnight, December 31, 1990 to be eligible.
3. Prizes: There will be ten (10) Grand Prizes awarded, each consisting of a choice of a trip for two people to: i) London, England (approximate retail value $5,050 U.S.); ii) England, Wales and Scotland (approximate retail value $6,400 U.S.); iii) Caribbean Cruise (approximate retail value $7,300 U.S.); iv) Hawaii (approximate retail value $ 9,550 U.S.); v) Greek Island Cruise in the Mediterranean (approximate retail value $12,250 U.S.); vi) France (approximate retail value $7,300 U.S.).
4. Any winner may choose to receive any trip or a cash alternative prize of $5,000.00 U.S. in lieu of the trip.
5. Odds of winning depend on number of entries received.
6. A random draw will be made by Nielsen Promotion Services, an independent judging organization on January 29, 1991, in Buffalo, N.Y., at 11:30 a.m. from all eligible entries received on or before the Contest Closing Date. Any Canadian entrants who are selected must correctly answer a time-limited, mathematical skill-testing question in order to win Quebec residents may submit any litigation respecting the conduct and awarding of a prize in this contest to the Régie des loteries et courses du Quebec.
7. Full contest rules may be obtained by sending a stamped, self-addressed envelope to "Passport to Romance Rules Request", P.O. Box 9998, Saint John, New Brunswick, E2L 4N4
8. Payment of taxes other than air and hotel taxes is the sole responsibility of the winner
9. Void where prohibited by law.

VACATION SWEEPSTAKES

Official Entry Form

MONTH 3 ENTRY

Yes, enter me in the drawing for one of ten Vacations-for-Two! If I'm a winner, I'll get my choice of any of the six different destinations being offered — and I won't have to decide until after I'm notified!

Return entries with invoice in envelope provided along with Daily Travel Allowance Voucher. Each book in your shipment has two entry forms — and the more you enter, the better your chance of winning!

Name _____

Address _____ Apt. _____

City _____ State/Prov. _____ Zip/Postal Code _____

Daytime phone number _____
                      Area Code

☐ I am enclosing a Daily Travel Allowance Voucher in the amount of $ _____ Write in amount revealed beneath scratch-off

---

VACATION SWEEPSTAKES

Official Entry Form

MONTH 3 ENTRY

Yes, enter me in the drawing for one of ten Vacations-for-Two! If I'm a winner, I'll get my choice of any of the six different destinations being offered — and I won't have to decide until after I'm notified!

Return entries with invoice in envelope provided along with Daily Travel Allowance Voucher. Each book in your shipment has two entry forms — and the more you enter, the better your chance of winning!

Name _____

Address _____ Apt. _____

City _____ State/Prov. _____ Zip/Postal Code _____

Daytime phone number _____
                      Area Code

☐ I am enclosing a Daily Travel Allowance Voucher in the amount of $ _____ Write in amount revealed beneath scratch-off

CPS-THREE